HAUNTED HOUSE

She'd left the door at the bottom standing open. Stepping out of the stairwell into the second floor hall, she began to turn around to close the door. A shadow spread across the floor and over her shoes. It moved as her head was swinging around, as her ears were acutely aware of a rustle like stiff cloth against dry skin, as her common sense woke screaming for the gym bag with its Mace, left behind in the kitchen. She felt the air sweeping ahead of the blow, felt the atmospheric compression before the moving solid object, and never felt the blow itself. . . .

Also by Carol Cail

Private Lies

UNSAFE KEEPING

CAROL CAIL

A DELL BOOK

Published by
Dell Publishing
a division of
Bantam Doubleday Dell Publishing Group, Inc.
1540 Broadway
New York, New York 10036

ISBN: 0-440-22298-2

Reprinted by arrangement with St. Martin's Press

Printed in the United States of America

Published simultaneously in Canada

October 1996

10 9 8 7 6 5 4 3 2 1

RAD

For my two sons, Matt and Todd—
you know who you are.

1

■ ■ ■

The traffic light turned yellow when Maxey was twenty yards from the intersection. Her right foot shilly-shallied between brake and accelerator while her mind did a quick calculation of the pros and cons of running it.

Almost midnight. No traffic. No pedestrians. Minor cross street. Her toe pointed at the accelerator.

On the other hand . . . Coming toward her from half a mile ahead was a vehicle the color and contour of a Boulder police car. Maxey's foot wavered left.

Ex-hubby Reece would never fail to run a stale yellow . . . Maxey stepped firmly on the brake.

As the Toyota coasted to a stop, two things happened. Her tape deck clicked over to a second side of Genesis, and a stealthy black shape catapulted left to right across her path.

''Uh,'' she said, flinching, grinding her shoe into the brake pedal of the already-stationary Toyota.

The blur became a panel van that cleared the intersection, didn't make the gentle bend in front of the University Memorial Center, jumped the curb, and uprooted four news racks and a mailbox.

Maxey's two hands clamped the steering wheel, vicariously steering the still-careening van. Phil Collins's drums began to wrap the Toyota in a seductive, inappropriate beat.

Dragging one ruptured news rack, the van lumbered across the grass and tackled a stocky cottonwood. The tree doubled over as if the wind had been knocked out of it. The van stopped dead.

Maxey shut her mouth and reached across the passenger seat to crank the window down. The soft May night slipped inside, smelling of lilacs, until it began to smell like gasoline. When she snapped off the tape player, she could hear the rustle of the wounded tree and a creaking of metal against metal.

White and red lights strafed the area as the patrol car that she'd spotted earlier reached the intersection, slid into the turn, and rocked to a stop. The siren burped one warning growl. Then the policeman was out of his vehicle, walking briskly toward the ruined van, his hand on his gun hip.

Maxey twisted her steering wheel hard right and parked the Toyota three feet from the curb. She was vaguely conscious of her heart and lungs dancing independent tangos as she grabbed notebook and pen from the next seat and swung her feet into the street.

The dragged news rack had skinned a path

through CU's young grass. Maxey followed it toward the policeman, who, hands cupped around his eyes, peered into the van's left-side window. All the glass was tinted the sinister opaque black that made Maxey glad she didn't have to pull strangers over for speeding. Hugging notebook to chest, she waited beside the back fender.

"See anyone?" she said.

Winding his fingers into the handle, the policeman lifted and pulled the door open. When he hauled himself inside and the door fell shut, Maxey converted a shudder into meaningful activity, opening her book and writing a description of the scene so far.

Damn it, why were her fingers so shaky? She'd witnessed worse smashups than this.

The van thumped and shivered and the back door banged aside, letting the policeman out.

"Get away from it," he said, striding back toward the street. "It could always explode."

Stumbling in his wake, she tried to catch a normal breath. "Is someone hurt in there?"

"Nobody in it."

"A runaway, huh?"

Opening the cruiser door, he reached in to the dashboard and hauled out a microphone. For the next several seconds, he talked to his dispatcher in numbers and acronyms.

The throbbing roof light changed his breast ID

from blood red to bleached white. T. D. Martinez. Maxey jotted it into her notebook and added a description of him: "Set mouth and blank eyes of a public servant doing his god-damn job."

Returning the mike to its cradle, he straightened, set one black shoe on the sill of his open door, and whipped out his own pocket notebook. "Could I please see your driver's license, ma'am?"

She had to hunt it out of the shoulder bag she'd left on the floor of the Toyota. Most driver's license pictures look like mug shots. Maxey's was taken the day she cut her blond hair herself, and she'd blinked her eyes at the wrong moment, so the photo looked like a crime-scene shot of the victim.

Handing the license to Martinez, she sucked in her stomach, hoping she could still pass for five foot four, 120 pounds.

"You were proceeding north on Broadway and had stopped at the Sixteenth Street intersection?"

She was very glad to be able to say yes. When she had the time to think about it, *glad* might be too mild a word.

The officer wandered a few steps away to get a reading on her license plate. "Mind telling me where you were going?" he called.

"Home." Though she didn't see that it had any bearing, she had nothing to hide. "I'd been at Chautauqua."

He walked back, lowering his voice. "To a concert or something?"

"I was interviewing the program director about the upcoming season."

"You a reporter?"

She nodded. "For the *Regard.*"

Maybe he'd smile now, recognizing her. Boulder County residents could be divided into two groups: those who were devout readers of the little alternative paper and those who had never heard of it.

Martinez didn't smile. He handed back her driver's license.

"Hey!" The voice was faint, but it kept getting louder. "Oh no. Oh no! What the—oh no."

A tall man jogged toward them down the Sixteenth Street hill. The streetlamps at the intersection gleamed on his balding head and transformed his vaguely sinister clothing into a dark navy shirt and slacks.

He panted to a stop beside the police cruiser and gaped at the mangle of van and tree.

The cop raked him with a practiced eye. "Is this your van, sir? May I see your driver's license?"

The man drew out a wallet and fumbled through it, muttering. "Somebody tried to steal it, right? Damn."

"There was no one in the vehicle. The parking brake is off and the gear's in neutral," Martinez said. "What does that suggest to you, sir?"

''I must've forgotten to put it in park. Jesus.'' He offered the license and abruptly bent over. Maxey backed away, expecting vomit on her shoes, but he was only holding his knees, catching his breath, muttering curses.

''Why don't you sit in the backseat here while I fill out the accident report.'' Martinez' inflection was command rather than question.

Hanging around the open door, Maxey jotted notes of her own: ''Kelly Sheffer—visiting friends half block up Sixteenth. No proof of insurance.''

When Martinez was through with him, Sheffer hauled himself out of the patrol car as if every joint needed grease. He started across the grass toward the wreckage.

''Don't go too close, on account of an explosion,'' Maxey advised, drifting after him.

''Where's the restore key when you need it?'' he mourned.

''Sorry?''

''The computer command that lets you cancel the last dumb thing you did.''

''Oh. Yeah, I see what you mean.'' She scribbled it into her notes.

''So you saw it happen, huh?'' He kicked at a divot the news rack had gouged.

''Yes. Too bad it was all over by the time you arrived. Since it's going to cost you, you should at least have gotten a few thrills out of it.''

His smile was a wince. "I'm just glad nobody was hurt. Thank God the light was red. You could've been killed. Look out—here's the tow truck."

Snapping the notebook shut, Maxey backed out of the way of the chirpy-springed truck jouncing across the lawn. Suddenly, she wasn't Maxey Burnell, star reporter. She was little Maxine Diane, sobered and shaken by some real or imagined close call.

As she stared into the dazzling cruiser beacon, she rubbed at the chill in her arms and relived that split second—the one where the traffic light switched to yellow and she had to choose the accelerator or the brake.

■

She drove home with exaggerated care, riding the brake pedal.

Finding a spot for the Toyota half a block from the apartment, she yanked up the parking brake, got out, locked up, and pressed her nose on the side window to double-check she'd engaged the parking brake.

Two cars hummed past in the time it took her to walk to the white Victorian three-story house. By day, Spruce Street busily accessed the center of town. By night, it was a drowsy, residential street.

A light glimmered deep in Mrs. Waterford's living room, reflecting on the gray-glossed porch floor. Maxey's landlady, a night person, usually played the

TV too loudly, well past Maxey's bedtime. Tonight the house lay quiet.

Crossing to the far west end of the porch, Maxey poked her key into the lock of her stair door and then paused, thinking about the silence. Mrs. Waterford had recently celebrated her eightieth birthday with a trip to Las Vegas—''Because it was there.'' Spry and independent, she was, nevertheless, a very senior citizen.

Backtracking to the screen door, Maxey rapped and called through it: ''Mrs. Waterford?''

What sounded like a kitchen chair scraping on wood flooring was followed by a reedy ''Yes?''

''It's Maxey. I was just coming home and saw your light.'' Now she'd have to borrow a cup of sugar or something. Mrs. W. wouldn't like the idea of being monitored.

''Come in, dear,'' came the summons, and, as Maxey found the door hooked, Mrs. Waterford's slow tread progressed through the house, from back to front. ''Oh, you can't—just a minute.'' She cruised across the living room, the floor creaking and her nyloned thighs swishing against one another. ''Come in, come in.'' She bumped the hook out of its loop.

Mrs. Waterford wasn't fat, but she was large—tall and big-boned. Even now, when she had old age for an excuse, she didn't stoop or slouch. Maxey could imagine the younger version of this dignified lady—

riding a bicycle, dancing the Charleston, driving a roadster, being called "a fine-looking woman" by male contemporaries.

Maxey had to look up at her to ask, "Would you mind if I write you a rent check tonight? Since we're coming up on the first?" That sounded more reasonable than needing to borrow cake ingredients at one o'clock in the morning.

"Why certainly, if you're that eager to give away your money," Mrs. Waterford said, leading the way toward the light. "There's someone I want you to meet."

Through the dining room archway, Maxey could see a corner of the kitchen table and a pair of blue-jeaned legs lounging beside it.

"We were having coffee," Mrs. Waterford said. "Don't you want a cup?" She didn't slow, setting a course for the range top, sure of the answer.

The jeans belonged to a young man, who nodded, serious-faced, at Maxey. She reflected the nod and the failure to smile.

"This is my grandson . . . Timmie. My upstairs neighbor, Maxey Burnell. She owns the *Blatant Regard.* You know, our wonderful little weekly newspaper." Having tipped a teaspoon of instant coffee into a white china cup, Mrs. W. splashed teakettle water over it. Now she offered it to Maxey on an almost-steady saucer.

''Hello.'' Maxey stretched out her free hand to the young man. ''Tim is it?''

''Timothy,'' he corrected, raising his backside a foot off the chair. He squeezed her hand. Finally, he smiled, and Maxey was reminded of a boy she'd known in high school—a slightly overweight, too pale artist, whose hair always needed combing and jaw always needed shaving, but whose smile was as sweet and warm as honey on home-baked bread.

Timothy wasn't going to lose any pounds today, judging by the Winchell's doughnuts box beside his left hand.

''You're the publisher of the *Regard*?'' he said. ''Hey, that's quite the controversial publication. Good job. Great job.''

Maxey thought she could like this kid. She sipped at the coffee, wondering if there were any doughnuts left.

''Sit down,'' Mrs. Waterford insisted, clearing magazines off one chair and a stack of folded laundry off another, as if Maxey might want a selection to choose from.

Settling on the closer chair, Maxey unzipped her shoulder bag to search out her checkbook. ''Do you live in Boulder, Timothy?''

''For now. I'm going to the university. Home is Colorado Springs.''

''Uh-huh. What are you studying?'' Maxey uncapped her roller-ball pen and squashed the checkbook flat to write.

"Just liberal arts for now. Can't make up my mind." He removed the Benjamin Franklin spectacles and rubbed at his eyes with thumb and forefinger. "I'm kind of leaning toward journalism."

"Oh?"

Mrs. Waterford had sat down at the far end of the table and was tracing the paisley pattern of the yellow oilcloth with one gnarled forefinger, her chin propped on the other long-boned hand. She said, "Timmie's dad—my son—was a sportswriter for the *Rocky Mountain News.*"

Maxey ripped out the check. "Gosh, I didn't know. Is he retired now?"

"Dead now," Timothy said. "Mom, too."

"I'm sorry to hear it," Maxey said, handing him the check to pass down to his grandmother. "Well, then you know not to get into the business expecting to make a fortune. I mean, some people do, but most don't."

"Yeah." Hooking the glasses back into place, Timothy smiled his angelic smile. "You making any money?"

"Nope."

"And proud of it, right?"

She glanced up, more startled than offended.

"Way to think," Timothy said. He offered one palm for a high five, and Maxey, grinning, lightly swatted it. Then Timothy frowned into his coffee cup. ''Me, I want to write, but I sure do hate being poor.''

''Have you been writing any freelance stuff?''

Nodding, he leaned away, all his weight on the twin hind legs of Mrs. W.'s antique chair. ''Science fiction, mostly. Some poetry.''

''And anything published?'' For right or wrong, this was the question that usually separated the scribes from the scribblers.

''Not yet. I will.'' He put the same heavy inflection on *will* that Reece had used when the minister asked if he'd love and honor till death. Maxey hoped Timothy's vow would stand up to time better than her ex's had.

Swallowing the last of her coffee, Maxey stood. ''Gotta leave. I gotta go to sleep so I can wake up.''

Mrs. Waterford insisted on seeing her to the door.

''I can find it.'' Maxey laughed. ''Or are you afraid I'll lift an antimacassar on the way out?''

''Oh, for heavens—if you want one, you're welcome to it,'' Mrs. Waterford assured her.

Trudging up the steep chute of stairs to her apartment, Maxey could hear Moe, closed in at the top, meowing her on.

''Coming, coming,'' she promised, thankful someone was glad to have her home, even if the gladness was mostly due to Maxey's skill at dispensing kitty surf 'n' turf.

The gray-and-white corpulent cat had been part of Maxey's inheritance from Jim Donovan, the founder of the *Regard.* Jim, her employer and friend for less than three years, had died ten months ago. Maxey still couldn't unlock the news-office door or scratch Moe's greedy little chin without feeling a pang of loss.

"Let's ask Ernestine for our phone messages, shall we?" Maxey said, punching the rewind button of the telephone answering machine as she reached for the can opener.

Scraping Moe's aromatic meal into his bowl, she grimaced as Reece's mellow baritone said, "Hey, boss." He knew how she hated to be called that—especially since, Jim having willed half the newspaper business to him, Reece was as much "boss" as Maxey.

"I won't be in until after noon tomorrow," Reece was saying. "I want to interview somebody somewhere about something."

Probably a broad in a boudoir about her vital statistics, she thought.

The answering machine beeped and another sonorous masculine voice began to speak. "This is the Boulder PD, Ms. Burnell. We got some information you were involved in a traffic incident tonight. I'd like to take you down for questioning, if it's not too late when you slink yourself home."

2

■ ■ ■

Maxey's personal representative of the Boulder PD raised up on one elbow and hauled the sheet over them both. Still sweaty from the previous twenty minutes' activity, Maxey moaned and kicked one foot free to what little air filtered past her bedroom curtains.

One more debt that Maxey owed to her late employer, Jim Donovan, was that he'd brought City Detective Sam Russell into her life. The investigating officer in Jim's unnatural death, Sam made Maxey feel very much alive.

Now tucking the sheet around his chest and under his armpits, Sam folded hands on waist and said, "That hit the spot."

"Don't say 'hit' to someone who was almost smashed by a runaway van tonight," Maxey mumbled.

"Yeah, let's talk about that."

"It's after two and I have to work tomorrow. What's to talk about?"

"Bet you didn't know it's happened three times before in the last month."

Maxey's eyes batted open in spite of herself. By her Mickey Mouse night-light, Sam's lean face was all chiseled planes and shadowed hollows. With one forefinger, she traced his mouth, prodding it into a smile.

"What's happened three times?" she asked.

"Runaway vehicle. Owner leaves it on a hill, unlocked; can't remember whether he put it in park. Late night, deserted street. Nobody hurt—yet."

The reporter in Maxey was now fully awake. "You mean it's no accident?"

"What does it sound like to you?"

"Like some idiot's going round releasing emergency brakes."

"Did you witness anyone else at the scene besides the van owner and Martinez? Any looky-lou getting his rocks off on the excitement?"

Maxey shut her eyes, the better to see the intersection, the soft night, the hard van. "Nobody."

"You want to do a public-service piece in the *Regard*, tell people to turn their wheels into the curb and lock their vehicles."

"Kids," Maxey decided, snuggling down to try for sleep again. "It's probably dumb kids."

■

In nice weather—which in Boulder, Colorado, is most of the time—Maxey walked to work. The newspaper office was less than seven blocks away, on Pearl Street's pedestrian mall. Friday morning dawned fine, but her late hours the night before felt like weights on all her limbs. Getting out of bed—especially since Sam didn't have to—was like trying to run in soft sand.

By the time she'd dragged on clothes and eaten a peanut butter sandwich breakfast, she had to drive or be late opening the office. The fact that she started the car, drove the six blocks, couldn't find a parking space, and settled for a space half the way home again did not amuse her.

The whole morning was more of the same. The coffeemaker expired and took a fuse with it. The mail lady delivered eight bills and a smutty-videotape catalog. Two irate readers telephoned to cancel their subscriptions, and one equally disgruntled advertiser canceled, all of them enumerating their reasons in full and in tedious duplicate. Reece, as promised, wasn't there to help her deal with any of this—not that he would have helped her if he had been there.

The Thursday paper was history now, and Maxey tried, under the dull threat of an oncoming headache, to plan next week's issue. The priority task was soliciting ads, but she hated that job. So did Reece, which meant there'd be the usual argument, coin flip, and him weaseling out if he lost.

What could she write about instead? Nucla's annual prairie-dog shoot? Small town provides small game for folks with small attention spans. She sat down and scribbled herself a note to call the town hall and get the usual "We're a poor area with no other way to attract tourists" whiny quote.

Gun control? It had been at least two weeks since her last editorial on the right not to bear an armed public. An article about gun control would fit nicely with one on Colorado's new stalking law.

Resting chin on hand, not worrying about how she looked with her cheek stretched toward her ear, Maxey noodled out a first paragraph for the stalker piece: "At last! The cops don't have to fold their arms and wait for old boyfriend to gun down the lady he adores. Now they can arrest him for following her too closely."

Her stomach growled, and she wished she'd climbed out of the apocryphal sand dune early enough that morning to make herself a brown-bag lunch. Maybe Sam was still in her bed. If she locked the office for an hour, she could rush home, tear off her clothes, belly flop into the sheets, and—

The front door rattled open. Sounds of the pedestrian mall leaked in—feet and voices and a guitar playing "Greensleeves." The person coming through the doorway was female, a stranger, young. She carried a clipboard crushed to her chest, and no purse. Maxey didn't analyze why this seemed like bad news.

"Hello," the woman said. "May I speak to you a minute?"

"Okay." Hands poised over the computer keyboard, Maxey hoped she looked too busy for a charitable solicitation but not too busy to accept a paid advertisement.

"I hoped you'd be interested in signing my petition." The woman crossed the room purposefully, her tennis shoes cheeping on the bare wood floor. "This is about the Gunderloy house." She whipped off her dark glasses and blinked her eyes, the color of weak tea.

"The Gunderloy house." Maxey frowned, and the headache that had been building below the surface broke in a wave behind her right eye.

"May I?" Dropping into the straight chair beside Maxey's desk, the woman lowered the clipboard from her bosom. "It was built in 1864 by Boulder's most exclusive madam."

"Madam." Maxey rubbed at her forehead.

Up close, the young woman was older—forty, probably. Her slender athletic build in the tan safari shirt and slacks made her seem younger than the skin around her eyes and mouth could pretend.

"Madame Fionna Estelle Gunderloy. Isn't that a

wonderful name? She had fifty girls at the peak of her business.''

For one wild moment, Maxey thought this was going to turn out to be a paying ad after all. ''I'm sorry, I don't see what—''

''Celia Vogle is my name, by the way.'' Celia bounced forward on the chair and offered a firm, dry handshake before continuing her narrative. ''The house is in surprisingly good shape. A gem. Queen Anne with just a dash of Italianate. A witch's hat tower roof, and you can imagine the graceful stairways and cunning little rooms, but all of it tastefully—''

''Could you please clarify what it is you want?'' Maxey had to interrupt. ''I'm afraid you've caught me at a bad time.''

''Oh, sorry. Well, our neighborhood group is trying to save the house.'' Celia laid the clipboard on Maxey's desk and tapped it meaningfully. ''We've already got over five hundred names on our petition.''

''Save?'' Maxey envisioned a run-down mansion full of born-again whores.

''From the wrecking ball. Skye and Skye Investments.'' Celia's thin mouth seemed to taste rotten meat. ''They want to build condos.''

''Why haven't I heard of any of this before?'' Maxey said, clutching the top of her head with both hands. It wasn't so much the historic house she was worried about as her own failure as a scout for the wagon train of current events.

"If it wasn't for the owner asking for Bailey Marker's advice, you still wouldn't know about it, and neither would the neighborhood group. Skye and Skye were trying to keep it all hush-hush until it was a fait accompli and too late for preservationists to act."

"Who's Bailey Marker?" Maxey asked, grabbing up a notepad and beginning, belatedly, to take notes.

"He lives right across the street from the Gunderloy. A dear old man. He used to play the saxophone in Tommy Dorsey's band." Celia watched Maxey write. "Are you going to put this in your paper? Oh, that would be wonderful."

"Where is this house?"

"The west end of Nebraska Street. Ha, surprised you, didn't I?" Celia wriggled back into her chair and folded her arms. "Not the historic part of town, is it? Canyon Boulevard was the red-light district when Boulder was new. Madame Gunderloy wisely divorced herself from that riffraff and built her mansion way to the north. It was just rabbit-brush and chokeberries then. No other houses for a mile. Didn't take too many years for the town to spread up and surround it, though."

Maxey was nodding and scribbling. "So who owns this house?"

"I don't know." Celia's eyebrows lifted to mirror

Maxey's skepticism. ''Bailey knows, but he's keeping it confidential for now. Says he doesn't want to cause her unnecessary fuss.''

''Well, it'll be easy enough to research at the courthouse,'' Maxey muttered, penning herself a reminder.

''I guess you're willing to sign our petition, huh?'' Celia nudged the clipboard a quarter inch nearer Maxey's hand.

''Sure.'' Picking it up, printing her name and address in the designated squares, Maxey said, ''If this is such a venerable old building, how come the city isn't taking the initiative to save it? We've got a Landmarks Commission.''

''Oh, I'm sure they'll help. But you can't force a property owner to register for landmark status. It's up to this female who owns it to decide whether to sell to the Skye boys, who have no interest in historic preservation whatsoever.''

''Old buildings aren't protected by any laws? Can't the state intercede for the public good or something?''

Celia was shaking her head. ''A man's home is his castle, is the way it's usually looked at. Even places like Philadelphia have had trouble saving landmarks after the Pennsylvania Supreme Court ruled that the city couldn't designate the Boyd Theater over the owner's objections. The court called it taking of private property without just compensation.''

Handing back the clipboard, Maxey could feel the story writing itself in her head. Remember history class? Can you name even one man who became famous because he demolished something?

The phone rang.

"Listen, I know you're busy, so I'll move along," Celia said, standing. "I'll watch for the write-up."

"Give me your phone number," Maxey said, scribbling it down before reaching for the telephone. "Thanks, Celia. Good luck." Snatching up the insistent receiver, she said, "*Blatant Regard*, Maxey Burnell."

"He threw it on the roof again," a quavery, angry voice told her as Celia slipped out the door.

"I believe you meant to dial the *Camera.* This is the *Regard.* We don't deliver door-to-door. I can give you the correct number to call." Maxey recited it from memory, having experienced mistaken-identity problems before.

Now the old woman was completely incensed. "Well, for—your trouble is, you've got too many extensions. How's a person to get the right department when there's so many phones?"

"Yes, ma'am. Why don't you give me your address, and I'll tell your carrier about the problem."

The front door opened and Reece's familiar silhouette briefly blanked out the sunlight. He crossed to his desk, a clutch of newspapers in one hand and a sweating soft-drink can in the other.

Holding the phone away from her ear, Maxey made a face at her ex-husband. ‘‘We’ve got to get an office person.’’

He settled one hip on the edge of the desk and tipped his head back to drink some Sprite, his throat gracefully undulating. He wore his usual work outfit: jeans, a T-shirt—this one basic black—and athletic shoes that had once been white and had mellowed to sepia. He was either in the early stages of growing his annual beard or he was temporarily out of razor blades.

Having found a hole in the *Camera* subscriber’s monologue big enough to insert a ‘‘good-bye,’’ Maxey hung up the receiver. ‘‘Whatever happened to our plan to get some office help?’’ she asked Reece. ‘‘We need someone to answer the phone and run errands and clean the rest room.’’

‘‘You mean you’d be willing to delegate some authority? Let a novice scour the john?’’ Reece pretended to be amazed.

Waiting in vain for her to laugh, he rubbed a palm down the back of his head. He was also, due to style or economy, letting his hair grow. No amount of negligence had yet affected his hunky body. It was a gift, because Reece didn’t have the get-up or the go to keep it that lean.

Maxey said, ‘‘We’ve run the *Regard* for almost a year now. We’ve got enough in the bank account to hire somebody at minimum wage—somebody who wants to learn the news biz.''

''An apprentice. A disciple,'' Reece emoted, assuming a spread-armed, wide-legged stance that implied he was about to begin chorus dancing with joyful abandon. ''A debutante whom I can drill.''

''Oh no you don't. No cute soufflés who don't know their *lie* from their *lay.*'' Maxey ripped the Gunderloy notes from her five-by-eight pad and began listing job qualifications on a clean page. ''We'll advertise the position in this week's *Regard.* And speaking of ads, I hope that's what you were doing this morning.''

''Aw, no, sorry.'' Without expanding on that, Reece hauled out his swivel chair and dropped into it, putting his back to her and an end to the discussion.

Maxey finished her help-wanted copy and slid her shoulder bag out of the desk drawer. ''I'm going to lunch.''

'' 'Kay.''

Circling past him, Maxey noticed he was reading their competitor's sports page. It reminded her she'd promised the *Camera*'s dissatisfied customer to pass along the word about the carrier's high, outside pitches. It would be easy to go west a block to do it in person, and then she'd have lunch at Pour La France across the street.

The brick walkway of Pearl Street Mall was

crowded with early-afternoon shoppers and sight-seers. Maxey nodded at a few familiar faces as she walked: the balloon man, torturing his squealing wares into pink spiders and red giraffes; the gaunt cowboy who played guitar, his scuffed instrument case yawning open to snap up spare change; the sad-faced man dressed in a dull-black tuxedo, washing windows at the bookstore with slow painstaking. A pigeon strutted across Maxey's path, his iridescent eye fixed sideways at her.

At Eleventh Street, easing across against the light, Maxey remembered her idea of going home for lunch, to check up on the policeman in her bed. But no, Sam would be long gone by now, either at his apartment or at the station.

She looked up from the curb, and there he was.

He was standing beside a lamppost, next to a concrete bowl that erupted petunias in primary colors. Dressed in the killer eggshell jeans and gray-blue work shirt Maxey had given him for his birthday, Sam looked like a page out of a Lands' End catalog. He didn't see her yet, his strong profile inclined toward his companion. Now Maxey noticed the woman.

Reece would have been so jealous. This cute soufflé was blond where she wasn't tanned. Her orange dress showed off a wonderfully flat stomach surrounded by rolling real estate. Her long legs winked in the sunlight as she shifted poses, cocking one little foot on its stiletto heel.

Maxey saw all this in the one second it took for her own foot to plant itself on the pavement and smartly swivel her into an about-face. Disregarding the DON'T WALK signs and the traffic rabbit-stopping around her, she strode back the way she'd come.

The woman was probably a witness, someone Sam was interviewing for a case in progress. He wasn't touching her, was he? No, but he was smiling. Taciturn Sam Russell was grinning like a wolf in grandma's clothing, his mouth braced to exclaim, Surprise.

Maxey's flat soles slammed her along the walkway past the *Regard* entrance, past every entrance on this block, and marched her across the next cross street. She and Sam had been lovers for almost ten months, and never had either suggested they should move in together. They certainly had no claim on each other. She had no right to feel this possessive.

This miserable.

She ought to confront Sam right now, find out exactly who this woman was. After all, how many relationships have crash-landed due to someone's ejecting from the wrong conclusions?

Finally, eventually, Maxey ran out of mall. Coming to the intersection of Pearl and hectic Fifteenth, she turned around and began retracing her route, strolling now, adrenaline depleted.

She sat down on a brick wall that imprisoned a mob of red geraniums. It occurred to her that she hadn't heard ''I love you'' in at least a year.

''Hey, Maxey. You look like you just lost your best friend,'' a male voice said above her head.

3

■ ■ ■

Maxey looked up reluctantly, longing to be left alone. Mrs. Waterford's grandson leaned his elbows on the handlebars of the ten-speed bike he'd been walking beside. His rugby shirt reflected bright red on the underside of his chin. His white shorts looked as if he'd spent a sleepless night in them.

"Hi. I recognized you in spite of the long face." Timothy's voice was casual, his eyes intent with avid curiosity.

"I've got a headache," Maxey said. It was the truth, if not the whole truth. She struggled to smile. "Shopping, are you?"

"Just mall crawling. Seeing and being seen. Have you had lunch yet?"

For a moment, she couldn't recall. "No, but I'm not hungry."

"Bet it would help your headache. Where's somewhere close and cheap I could take you?" Timothy, twisting to survey the walkway, noticed a sleek Corvette at the cross-street light and lost his train of thought.

Feeling old, Maxey watched him admire the car. He'd shaved, and his hair was washed and combed, but he had a just-wakened look, his eyes puffy behind the Franklin spectacles.

"How about a pizza?" he finally said as the Corvette gunned away.

"I'll be fine, Timothy, thanks all the same. You don't have to—"

"Yeah, I do. Come on." He clasped her elbow and gently lifted, as if she were his grandmother trapped in a too-low overstuffed chair.

Oh hell. Maybe a sandwich would ease the physical pain at least. They strolled west, the bicycle between them. She scanned the route for fickle policemen.

"There's a good deli along here," she said. She squinted at a bright orange dot far ahead, trying unsuccessfully to see a gray-and-white dot beside it.

"Which way's the *Regard* office? Maybe after we eat, you'd give me a tour of it."

"That would take all of sixty seconds."

"Whoa, I'm not your average tourist. I can ask intelligent questions, like where's your clip art library and how much rubber cement do you use in a month."

Now Maxey could see that the orange dot was not a dress but a baby's stroller.

"Is this the place?" Timothy prompted, and nodding, she waited for him to chain the bike to a lamppost. Leaving the sunlight, they stepped into the white-and-chrome ambience of the Dilly Deli.

Everything about the place always gleamed, including owner Morrie's forehead, which was relentlessly expanding toward the half-dollar bald spot on the top of his head. He was wiping off a table, the weight of his big body making it creak and sway.

"Hey, Maxey," he said in his surprisingly soft voice.

"Hey, Morrie. What's the special today?" She slid out a white wire chair beside the table he was working on and waited for him to finish before sitting down.

"Reuben. Choice of corned beef, pastrami, or turkey." Morrie's friendly golden face with its ripe-banana freckles swung around to notice Timothy.

"Yum," Maxey said. "Make mine pastrami."

Timothy studied the menu board behind the glass refrigerated case across the room. "Tuna melt and a Coke." He scraped out the other chair and sat.

Maxey was glad they were too early for the noon rush. Through the window beside her shoulder, she monitored the passing foot traffic, watching for Sam. Maybe the blonde was his sister. He had one sister, in Little Rock or some other place that Maxey had never been.

Timothy leaned back in his chair and began to peel

paper off a straw in readiness for the forthcoming cola. Maybe Sam would happen to see Maxey with this male stranger and jump to conclusions of his own.

No, Timothy was too young. He chewed on the unwrapped straw, an arm flung over the back of the chair, pretending nonchalance or actually suffering boredom. Maxey didn't feel as if she was a date; she felt dated.

Morrie's teenaged waiter delivered Timothy's Coke and Maxey's iced tea, her usual, which had gone without saying.

Having talked her into lunch, Timothy now seemed disinclined to underpin his share of a conversation. They both stared out the window, a pair of morose bookends, until the sandwiches arrived.

"So has summer school started?" Maxey asked before biting into the fragrant stack of meat and bread.

"Uh-huh." Timothy lifted the toast roof of his sandwich to examine what was inside.

"Where are you living?"

He shot her an odd look, a mixture of embarrassment and irritation. "Grandmother's extra bedroom, for now."

"Sure. Reasonable housing is hard to find," she sympathized. Still, in the summertime there were usually plenty of vacant apartments.

"I need to get a part-time job," Timothy said. It was the universal lament of college students.

"I expect your grandmother is happy to have you in the house, for a while at least. To carry out the garbage and go after groceries and such." Maxey said this to inspire him, in case he wasn't already doing his share.

"Mmm," he said, mouth full.

"Hey, Maxey," Morrie called across the take-out showcase as he scooped coleslaw into cardboard buckets. "What's this I hear about you on KUCB today?"

"I don't know," she answered, startled. "Something I can sue them for?"

"Witness to an auto accident." He slammed the sliding door and opened a different one, reaching for fruit salad. "Lucky you weren't hurt."

"Yeah. Sam says there's a rash of runaway vehicles lately." She lowered her voice to say to Timothy, "Which reminds me. I need to write a cautionary editorial about that."

"A bunch of people forgetting to set their brakes?" Timothy said, fighting a string of melted cheese that stretched between bread and mouth.

"My policeman friend thinks some pin brain is going around releasing emergency brakes for the heck of it."

He put the sandwich down and stared at her. "Yeah? What a dumb thing to do."

Since he seemed interested, she told him about stopping for the yellow light in time to watch the at-large van become embedded in CU's tree. Timothy shook his head, properly aghast at Maxey's narrow escape.

The school clock above the outside door clicked to high noon, and within five minutes all the tables were occupied. The quiet disappeared under buzzing voices, clattering flatware, the ringing of the cash register.

Maxey and Timothy split the check—darned if she was going to pay for Timothy's when it had been his idea—and were almost to the door when it swung outward and she saw Reece standing there, motioning a young woman to enter in front of him.

Maxey backed into Timothy, letting them in. "You couldn't have waited another five minutes for my lunch half-hour to be over? So the office wouldn't be closed in the middle of the day?" she complained.

"Nice to see you, too, partner," Reece said, dropping a hearty hand on her shoulder. "Here, meet Rachel. Rachel, Maxey."

Another blonde in a miniskirted dress—blue, this time. She smiled at Maxey without opening her mouth, eyes heavy with mascara and indifference. Maxey's snap judgment, biased by recent events having nothing to do with Rachel, was that this was a hussy if ever she'd seen one.

That, of course, explained why Reece had put his

hand in the small of Rachel's back and was grinning like a cat on his way to swallow a canary.

"Nice to meet you," Maxey lied, easing around them to reach the door. Timothy eased with her, though she could sense his perfect willingness to stay and talk awhile. He gave the impression of straightening his clothes and slicking his hair, although actually he hadn't done either.

"Grab a table," Reece told Rachel. "I'll be right there. Talk to you a minute, Maxey?" And he followed them outside.

"Reece, this is Timothy Waterford. He's my landlady's grandson."

The two men performed a quick handshake. Timothy backed away three feet and openly listened for whatever came next.

"Uhh, Maxey, you know what we were talking about this morning? Hiring office help?"

She groaned out loud. "Don't say it. Please don't say what I think you're going to say."

"Rachel's got news-office experience. She worked the want-ad desk at the Longmont *Times Call* straight out of high school."

"Oh? She's out of high school? Isn't that a little older than you usually prefer?"

"Come on, Maxey. Don't let jealousy interfere with—"

"Jealousy! What have I got to be jealous about? I'm good-looking. I'm smart. I'm a superfine journalist. And it sure isn't you who would make me jealous, because I don't give one good damn anymore how many females you process through your bed-and-breakfast mill.''

Reece pulled back, chin tucked into his neck, looking truly shocked. As well he might. Maxey hadn't lost her temper like this since before their divorce more than three years ago. They'd become such good friends, he'd probably forgotten they were ever lovers.

Maxey, meanwhile, felt the stinging behind her eyes that indicated she'd better get the hell out of here before she made an even larger fool of herself.

Reece said, ''Well, sure, we don't have to decide right this minute.''

''Oh, but we have decided,'' she said. ''Not Rachel. Not anyone who looks and smells like a ripe passion fruit. Because I've already decided that Timothy would be perfect for the job, and I think, after you've interviewed him, you'll agree.''

The fact that Timothy did not allow his mouth to drop open or his eyebrows to climb into his bangs impressed and gratified Maxey. As smoothly as if she had indeed discussed employment opportunities with him, he said, ''I really do need the money, sir.''

People trying to enter the deli had gradually displaced the three, until now they were standing in the shade of a locust tree in the median of the mall.

Picturing Rachel's growing impatience as she

waited for Reece to "be right there," Maxey egged him on. "Go ahead. Ask Timothy something that a prospective employee ought to know."

Reece pursed his lips and considered Timothy, who didn't cringe or fidget. "Okay, Waterford, are you going to lie or lay down on the job?"

"I'm going to lie down on the job," Timothy declared without hesitation. He folded his arms, his eyes alert and amused.

"What's the possessive case of *it*?"

"*I-t*—no apostrophe—*s*. Unless you mean the big fur ball on *The Addams Family*, in which case the spelling would be capital *I-t*—apostrophe—*s*."

"By Jove, I think he's got it," Maxey said, delighted to discover that Timothy's job qualifications included intelligence as well as neediness.

Reece jumped as if stung, glanced at his watch, and started toward the deli. "I get one more question. Don't either of you sign anything till I've thought this over during lunch."

Maxey and Timothy reached the *Regard* office without encountering Sam. Since Timothy didn't know they were watching for somebody, he was the one who was not both relieved and disappointed.

■

It would be on his mother's head. It was her fault for wanting him to mow the grass.

Ronald Ramon Tilton—Tilt to his friends and enemies—crouched over the power mower, watching the gasoline gurgle into it from the grimy five-gallon can, and the smell seeped into his mind, deciding him.

Thunking the can on the concrete garage floor, Tilt stared at it the way an alcoholic stares at the siren bottle. He'd been home four months, plenty long enough for boredom and resentment to set in. He believed he deserved some pleasure after all those weeks in rehab and, before that, prison.

Automatically, he screwed the caps on the gas tank and gas can, moved the throttle down, yanked the cord. The mower howled and Tilt pointed it into the yard.

The amount in the can was enough for tonight; he'd already set his heart on tonight. He had never aspired to fancy strategy—no delayed touch-offs, no candles in shredded packing in attics, no wicks trailered to water-heater burners, no electronics. He had never cared whether the fire was recognized as arson or not. Tilt's style was to break in, slop the combustible around, dribble a path to ignite with a cigarette, run.

Following the mower in smaller and smaller squares, he was miles away, mentally driving familiar streets, looking for a likely spot. The old requirements would still apply: an empty house, off the beaten track, mostly frame, not too close to any neighbor.

His mother came out on the porch and began waving her flabby arms. It could mean anything from "Lunch is ready" to "You missed a spot over there." He pretended not to see her, and after a minute, she went inside.

Finishing the front, he circled toward the bald and weedy backyard. The mower brayed louder as he passed between the house and the garage. Twelve hours from now, he'd be slipping along here in the dark, swinging the gasoline can into his hand without a chink of sound, unlocking his old Chevy at the front curb, leaving the lights off till he was halfway down the block. He felt the unfamiliar curl of his lips that meant he was smiling.

When he finished mowing and came into the kitchen for a glass of water and a cigarette, his mother wandered in from the front room. Wiping at her nose with a tissue that she then stuffed inside a sleeve, she said, "You had a phone call. Some young woman who said she knows you at the university. The number's by the phone."

"What's her name?" Tilt wasn't much interested. There weren't any young women in any of his classes that he wanted to know better—or men, either.

"I don't remember. You'll have to look. She wanted to ask you something about an assignment." His mother waited in the doorway, everything sagging and her hair as gray and greasy as smoke. "You want me to bring the note out here?"

"No. Just forget about it, can't you? Don't worry about it."

She stared at him a steady half minute to show how hurt she was, and then she shuffled away down the hall.

Tilt let the smile stretch his mouth again, laughing at himself for feeling turned on, for needing no better lover than his own two hands. He sipped water, anticipating tonight, when he would literally light his own fire.

■

Reece's third question to Timothy was, "Smoking or non-smoking?"

"I'm not a smoker, but I'm a chain-eater," Timothy admitted, rubbing his belly.

"You a good cook?" Reece speculated. "We could always use some coffee cake around here first thing in the morning."

"Sorry. My specialty is burnt toast."

Reece had come back from the deli without Rachel. Maxey was dying to ask him how Ms. Congeniality had reacted to his returning to their table late and barren of job offers.

"Did Maxey tell you how paltry the wages are?"

"They beat the zip I'm earning now."

"Timothy has classes five mornings a week, but

he can work afternoons. And Saturdays, if need be,'' Maxey said. ''He can have my old desk if you'll be so good as to scrape all your overflow junk off of it.''

Maxey had appropriated Jim's computer desk after he died. Now she sat down at it to ward off Reece, who, having obediently scooped up an armload of assorted correspondence, was looking for a dumping place. She realized that her headache had dematerialized.

Beaming, Timothy tried out the rolling chair that went with his new work space. ''I can start right away. Give me something to do.''

Maxey leaned sideways to extract a scrap of paper from her skirt pocket. ''Here. Go over and tell the *Camera* that they threw it on the roof again.''

4

■ ■ ■

Tilt cruised from block to block, studying each cross street as best he could in the badly lit dark, till he ran out of cross streets. Well, hell, now he remembered the one he wanted was a T, not a four-way intersection. When he turned left, his headlights picked up the street sign confirming it: NEBRASKA.

He'd found his target that afternoon on the pretext of going after razor blades. Instead of driving to the shopping center drugstore, he'd toured residential neighborhoods, not afraid to be seen studying the places marked for sale—just another prospective buyer eyeing the merchandise. He'd found this perfect beauty almost right away.

Nebraska was one of those mishmash streets with a little forties bungalow here, a big brick Victorian there, an immaculate lawn at one place and a wasteland of neglect next door.

His house choice wasn't for sale, or else the sign had been swallowed by the undergrowth. It was boarded up and bounded on three sides by plank fencing and unruly bushes. Nebraska ran smack dead into a foothill a few feet past it, and the nearest streetlamp stood three doors back. His reconnoitering done, Tilt had quietly U-turned the Chevrolet and glided away without seeing a single neighbor or, he was fairly confident, being noticed himself.

Now Tilt had returned, even less visible than before—black car, black clothing, black shadows all around. Pleased to find numerous cars parked along the street as cover for his own, he shut off the motor and listened to the neighborhood sleep.

After five minutes of hearing distant traffic, more distant airplanes, and one relentlessly barking dog perhaps a block away, Tilt rustled into position to unlatch his door gradually and lift his legs outside. He braced himself to draw the gas can from behind the seat, everything still charcoal dim, because, of course, he'd unscrewed the interior dome light.

Backing away, helping the door click shut, Tilt grinned up at the stars. Stiff-armed, not allowing the can's handle to clank, he carried the fuel as far as the side yard and set it in the shadow of a fat, prickly bush. Then he walked along the house, staring up at it.

It was bigger than it appeared from the street, maybe four times deeper than it was wide. The plywood-covered windows looked more impenetrable than the splintered gray siding of the walls. Turning the corner into the rear yard, Tilt dug his deliberately weak flashlight out of his pocket and thumbed it a quick on and off again at the porch.

In the afterimage on his closed eyelids, he saw the back door hanging crooked in its frame, its single window now a scrap of Sinclair sign, a caved-in spot right where the doorknob should have been.

Tilt crossed over to the lumpy stone-slab step, flashed his light again, and snorted at how easy this was. Somebody had recently broken in and somebody else had covered the damage with a temporary hasp and padlock. Tilt could have kicked it loose, if he hadn't minded the noise.

Instead, he went back to the Chevy for the crowbar, retrieved the gas can on his return trip, and was inside the house in less than three minutes.

The kitchen smelled of dry rot and mice. Setting the can down, Tilt strolled into the next room and the next, inspecting his surroundings by the glow of the flashlight muffled in the tail of his T-shirt. This was part of the ritual. Look the place over, not necessarily with an eye to where and how to start the fire, but just because it was interesting to prowl through a strange, empty house.

Dining room, yeah. Narrow little hall with built-in cupboards. Tilt opened a couple of drawers and doors and paused to scan the 1959 *Denver Post* lining one of them. He'd have been three then. Three—Christ, ancient history—the same year that his dad had split.

Tilt moved on to the next room—parlor, with a fireplace and straggly gray lace curtains. His granny's house had worn this kind of curtains, even down to the grimy color. Not much of a housekeeper, but boy could she bake gingerbread and cinnamon cookies and those little chocolate things glued together with icing. Tilt's mouth was suddenly washed with saliva, and he had to laugh as he spit at the fireplace. Above the mantel, a milky mirror reflected his face, lit from below and eerie, like the guy on the wall in Snow White.

God, this was better than a carnival.

He took a box of kitchen matches out of his pants pocket and used one to light a cigarette. Waving the flame out, he tucked the matchstick behind his ear and walked on.

Another room, another. Stairs. Bedrooms, bathroom, closets, more stairs, attic.

And then he went down to the basement, stone walls black with coal dust, the floor a rich red dirt you could grow flowers in if they didn't need photosynthesis. Under the musty stairway, Tilt found a mason jar of pickles, probably, the liquid as murky and lethal-looking as swamp water. He sidearmed it at the stone wall, and the jar caved in on itself, releasing a sweet and sour halitosis.

Tilt gave the cellar one last sweeping glance, imagining how it was going to look tomorrow with the sunshine streaming into all the corners and people standing on the edges, looking down.

Then he went upstairs to get the gas can, a little sorry, as usual, that the foreplay was over.

■

Saturday mornings, Maxey had a standing date with three Maytags at the do-it-yourself laundry. Monday had been traditional wash day while she was growing up, but that was because her mother hadn't worked outside the home five days a week. Looking back, Maxey couldn't remember her mother working inside the home, either. Maybe that helped to explain Maxey's father's running off to be a racecar driver when Maxey was six. She'd always resented his preferring automobiles to children—or at least to one child—but now that she was grown and had no desire whatsoever for offspring of her own, she was less critical of her sire's defection.

Collecting dirty laundry, detergent, and enough quarters to turn her purse into a lethal weapon, she descended to her Toyota.

The sky was busy with a variety of clouds, including the kind Maxey thought of as dry rain, the shower visible below the blue-gray mass like a wispy hula skirt, evaporating before any drops reached the ground.

The laundry project proved uneventful except for a new cotton knit skirt that came out of the dryer resized into a slipcover for a toaster oven. Loading the clothes, now as warm and fragrant as freshly baked biscuits, into the car again, Maxey debated whether to go straight home.

She didn't need groceries or gasoline or library books. She definitely wasn't going to hunt up Sam; he would have to make the next move. On the other hand, she didn't intend to sit at home waiting for Sam to et cetera, et cetera.

Pulling out of the parking space into traffic, she immediately had to brake for a light, and her eyes wandered to the license plate of the Thunderbird in front of her. Nebraska.

That's what she'd do—drive over to Nebraska Street and take a look at Madame Gunderloy's house.

She turned right and left and right again, working her way into the northwest corner of town. The east-west streets began to slope up to meet the foothills. The houses eclipsed by big old trees weren't fancy, but comfortable-looking, inviting.

Maxey hunched forward to read a corner sign and, muttering, "Nebraska," turned west on the narrow street. A tenth of a mile ahead, a four-story cottonwood tree wearing the remains of a plank tree house marked the end of the line.

Idling toward it, the Toyota bobbed across a drainage gully in the pavement. Cars parked intermittently along the sides narrowed the street down to one lane.

In the shade of the cottonwood barricade was a white automobile with CITY OF BOULDER, FIRE DEPT. on the side.

Maxey could see that it had come on official business. The last house on the south side was patent-leather black, and the remnants of its roof had dropped down around its second floor. Yellow plastic police tape had been tied between elderly twin maples on either side of the buckled front walk.

Maxey swooped the Toyota in at the curb, behind the fire department car, and rummaged through the glove compartment for her notebook before jumping out.

She hesitated only seconds before ducking under the tape. Listening for whoever else was here, she scouted around the side of the house. Now she realized that the front of the house, like an old western storefront, gave a false impression of what was behind. The fire had eaten away all the other walls. Maxey found herself at the edge of debris, staring into a tangle of plumbing, wiring, and bricks, where a broad-shouldered man in jeans and a rolled-sleeved blue shirt was bent over, photographing the remains of the floor.

Waiting till the shutter had snapped, Maxey said, "Hello?"

The man turned from the waist, booted feet still planted in the ruin, and raised his eyebrows. "Yes?"

"Excuse me. I'm Maxey Burnell of the *Blatant Regard.* Could I ask you a few questions?"

He stared off into the backyard while he thought about it, and Maxey studied his nicely compact derriere. His hair was the color of middle-aged shake shingles, brown going on gray, but there was still plenty of it, lifting gently in a downslope breeze.

Turning, he picked his way toward her, and now she noticed the mustache and the smile tracks at the corners of his eyes. For the moment, the smile wasn't otherwise evident.

"What did you want to know?"

"For starters, you are—"

"Calen Taylor. *C-a-l-e-n*," he added when she whipped up the notepad to write. "Investigator for the Boulder FD." He didn't offer to shake hands, his being enclosed in gray rubber gloves.

"So you're trying to determine the cause of this fire. When did it occur?"

"Early this morning. Around two, two-fifteen."

"What's the address? Oh my gosh! This isn't the Gunderloy place, is it?" she said, stepping backward, trying to see the house across the street, looking for witch's hat roofs.

"Uh, I don't think so. Nobody lives here right now. First Bank owns it."

"Okay," she said, hoping for Celia's sake this wasn't the remains of the Gunderloy. "So do you know yet what started the fire?"

"Come over here. I'll show you." He offered his forearm to help her step up and over the stone foundation and onto the gritty black flooring.

"Is this safe to walk on?" she asked, feeling the illogical urge to tiptoe.

"Probably."

He guided her to the spot he'd been photographing. He squatted, knees popping, to point at a mark on the floor. Maxey studied the swirl of black that stood out against the charcoal surrounding it. With the point of a pocketknife, Calen hacked loose a scrap of the darkened carpet and offered it up to her.

"Smell."

Obediently, she sniffed. "It smells like the last time I barbecued hamburgers."

He grunted. "It's probably imagination, but I think I can still smell the gasoline. The lab will test this and tell us for sure. The pattern on the floor is typical of the way gasoline looks, slopped out of a can. When it burns, the greater heat it generates brands the surface."

"Ohh . . ." Maxey said, enlightened. "So this was arson."

"Not much question."

"Now how do you find out who?"

He grimaced, straightening up. "That's where it gets harder. Even if we've got a suspect, we have to have corpus delicti."

Maxey scribbled in her book. "I thought *corpus delicti* meant a murder victim."

"*Corpus delicti* means 'body of the crime.' If we want to prove beyond a reasonable doubt that someone committed arson, we have to have an eyewitness or a confession. Failing that, we need some superstupendous circumstantial evidence."

"Uh-huh, uh-huh," Maxey said, abbreviating to write it all down fast enough. "What kind of evidence?"

Calen cocked hands on hips, watching her write. "Say that our suspect has a motive, like he's the owner and needs the insurance money. Say he was seen in the vicinity right before the fire was discovered. Say we accuse him of setting the fire on purpose and he doesn't say anything one way or another. Any or, preferably, all of these things might convince a jury to bring in a guilty verdict."

"So do you have any or, preferably, all of these things?" Maxey looked up expectantly.

She was just in time to see the beginning smile at the edges of his mouth. It grew and crinkled his eyes, warping his whole face into an infectious happiness.

"I think I've got a fingerprint," he said.

"Yeah?" Maxey grinned, too. "On what?"

"If you promise not to break a leg and sue the city, I'll show you."

"Gentlewoman's agreement," she said.

He motioned her toward the remains of a stairwell

that led to the basement. Debris had been piled to one side of the stone risers, providing a path, if one didn't mind going down sideways and on one's toes.

"Suppose I'm an arsonist," Maxey remarked to the top of her guide's head. "What kind of person am I?"

"If you set a fire using gasoline, you're either an idiot or you've got a death wish. Gasoline explodes. You pour it around, fumble out a match, maybe splash around some more in some places that you missed. The fumes build up. First spark, and whomp, you're a fireball blowing out through the nearest wall."

Having reached the bottom of the stairs, Calen dragged a charred board out of the way and held up a cautionary hand. "Stay there a minute. I haven't photographed this yet."

He dug his little camera out of his shirt pocket, yanked up the flash, took three pictures from as many angles, and then motioned Maxey forward. They both stared down at a broken jar of—Maxey inhaled deeply—pickles. Calen took a needle-nosed pliers and a brown paper bag from another pocket and knelt to pick up a shard of the glass.

"See here?" He brushed heads with Maxey to share a patch of sunlight. "Not much, but you can see where his thumb or something impressed on the dust on the jar. A fresh fingerprint. If he was wearing gloves, they had a hole in them."

Maxey didn't think the tiny mark was much to brag about, but since it obviously had made Calen's day, she tried to be enthusiastic. ''So you can track him down by that?''

''Mmm, no. But if we get a suspect, and if any of his fingers match this pattern, it'll be better than circumstantial.'' Snapping the sack open, Calen deposited the evidence in it. ''So am I going to read about myself in the paper this week?'' He hunkered down and began tweezing up the rest of the jar.

''Bet on it. Who phoned in the fire alarm?''

''Old gent next door. Somebody Bailey.''

''Bailey Marker. You aren't going to take any of the pickles?'' she joked as Calen stood up and labeled the bag with a felt-tip pen from his trusty pockets.

''No, but I'll take their picture again,'' he said, and did. ''We have to have before and after pictures of everything—in case we get to court.''

''You need a search warrant to do this?'' Maxey asked, beginning to pick her way back upstairs.

''Sometimes—if the owner objects. The bank didn't, of course.''

Maxey paused at the top to give Calen a chance to go around and show her to the exit. ''Listen, I appreciate you taking the time,'' she said. ''Have you got a card?''

He patted all his pockets.

''That's okay, just give me your phone number,''

Maxey said. It was great to have a job where she could legitimately ask good-looking guys for their phone numbers.

He recited his, stripping off the rubber gloves. "Nice talking to you," he also recited, offering his right hand in a brisk, brief shake.

Maxey strode off, glad to be on terra firma again and away from the pervasive scent of scorched lumber.

Next stop, Bailey Marker.

5

■ ■ ■

As it turned out, Bailey Marker wasn't next, because coming around to the front of the fire scene, Maxey saw, straight ahead across the street, an unmistakable black shingle witch hat perched on a three-story tower.

Crossing toward it, she stopped every few steps to jot a note into her memo book. "Front porch—veranda?—wraps around on south side. Wedgwood blue wood frame trimmed in white. Steep, multiangled black roof. Columned balcony on second-story front. Dormers. Chimneys. Lots of arch-shaped windows. A house fit for a princess. Or maybe for a governess in search of a moody husband."

Maxey stopped short of the pink stone steps and peered at the front door, once probably a brilliant red and now faded to a jaundiced rose. She wondered if any of Boulder's founding fathers' fingerprints still layered the doorknob.

"Could I help you?" The voice was tenor, with a hint of southern drawl in it.

Twisting around, Maxey knew at once, for no good reason, that this was Bailey Marker. He was probably seventy or so, a tall man with white hair and a wide, bony forehead. His posture was both straight and casual, arms hanging loosely at his sides, as if he were a suit hanging from a closet rod.

"Hello," Maxey said, smiling. "Celia Vogle sent me."

"Celie? I guess you're not here to throw rocks through the windows, then."

They exchanged names. Bailey's fingers, skeletal and brittle-looking, gripped Maxey's in a strong handshake.

"What a great old house," she said, turning back to reexamine it.

"Needs work, but don't we all."

"I told Celia I'd run something about it in the *Regard.*"

"Oh, I see. Well, you tell the world we don't want a condominium here." He fumbled a white handkerchief from his back pocket and bugled his nose.

"Have you told the owner that? I understand you know her."

"Oh, yes, I passed along all the neighbors' comments to her after censoring some of them first. She's a decent gal. I think she'll do the right thing."

"Which is—"

"Which is to not sell out to Skye and Skye. Let the Landmarks Commission decide if the place can be designated a historical nugget. If she wants to sell—and she hadn't made any effort to do that till these Skye people started twisting her arm—she can surely find some private party with enough financing to make it livable."

"Could I have the owner's name?"

"Nope." He swung away to gaze into the distance. Case closed.

"How long has the place been vacant?"

"Le'see. Last renters—can't think of their name, but it must have been about five years ago."

Maxey surveyed the closely trimmed grass, the intact windows, the general state of repair. "The owner's maintaining it well."

"Yes, well, like I said, she's basically good-intentioned. She inherited the place from her dad, and she never needed or much wanted it, but it probably helps her income-tax situation. Vacant, I mean."

A motor started on the street, and both Maxey and Bailey turned toward the sound. Calen Taylor pulled away in his official car, waving without looking at them.

"You had some excitement this morning," Maxey said.

"Could have toasted you a few marshmallows," Bailey agreed.

A squirrel the color of caramelized carrots came

down the nearest cottonwood tree, around and around the trunk as if on a circular stairway. He perched astride an exposed root and gave the intruders sidelong looks.

"Okay if we walk into the backyard?" Maxey asked Bailey, already strolling in that direction. "How did you happen to discover the fire? Weren't you asleep?"

"When you get to be my age," Bailey said, his mouth twitching around a grin, "you get a lot of exercise with your sleep—getting up to go to the bathroom. Mine overlooks the scene of the crime. The frosted window was closed, but the glow of the flames showed up on it. My first thought was, Dang, some business is moving in over there and they got a neon sign. You know the dumb things you think when you wake up in the middle of the night."

"So you opened the window."

"And black smoke was just a-boiling out of the fire. Even in the dark, you could see the blackness of the smoke. I ran downstairs. Well, I walked fast downstairs," he amended. "Phoned the fire department, and they were here less than five minutes later. They gave my place a good bath, but I don't think it was ever in any real danger of catching."

"Did you see anyone? Who could have set it, I mean."

"No. I do think I heard a car start, just before I got up to . . . conduct my business."

They had reached the rear of the Gunderloy house, and Maxey shaded her eyes to squint at the upper stories. A deserted bird's nest was wedged in the rafters of a skimpy back porch.

''Is the owner a descendent of Madam Gunderloy's?'' Maxey stepped up on the creaky porch floor.

''I don't know the way of it,'' Bailey said. ''Seems I recall the madam didn't have any kin and left it to some friend or other.''

Maxey cupped hands to eyes and leaned into the speckled windowpane of the back door. She could see an old-fashioned white cupboard, a sink bowl with all its plumbing hanging out below, and a wire flyswatter suspended from a nail on the peely-papered wall. She tried, unsuccessfully, to see the lounging shapes of silk-wrapped ghosts, their charcoaled eyes dull with disillusionment.

''We don't want to romanticize the prostitution,'' she mused out loud, ''but the house itself deserves careful consideration.''

''That's the ticket.'' Bailey bent to rip out a patch of bindweed that was trespassing on the porch steps. ''Old isn't automatically bad. Old is just mostly inconvenient,'' he said, trying to straighten up again.

■

''Ronald Ramon.'' His mother's quavery voice floated up the stairs to him.

Tilt burrowed deeper into his pillow, grasping at a dream that was already out of range.

"Ronald Ramon!"

Groaning, he popped open one eye. His digital alarm clock registered 11:54. Sunlight and an intermittent breeze leaked under the flopping window shade. Tilt smacked his mouth and rolled up on an elbow.

"What? What do you want?"

"There's a phone call for you."

"Oh fer—Can't you take a message?"

"The gentleman says it's urgent."

"Okay, okay. I'm coming."

He slung away the covers and grabbed up the jeans he'd left on the floor. Muttering while he hauled up and zipped, he tramped barefoot into the hall. Probably some frigging siding salesman. Some family-portrait special offer. He'd flay their ears.

His mother had left the receiver on the little hall table and gone back to the kitchen. She had the TV on out there to some game show—fanfares and applause and an emcee too happy to be true.

"Yeah?" Tilt said into the phone.

"Tilton. I caught your act last night."

Muzzy-headed, Tilt frowned and wiped one hand down his face from eyes to whiskery chin. "Who is this?"

"A friend. I recognized you on Nebraska Street shortly before the fire trucks came. I think we could do some business. You could always use some tax-free dollars, right?''

By now, Tilt was stone-cold awake. Turning his back to the electronic pandemonium in the kitchen, he lowered his voice. ''If you don't tell me who you are and what you want in short, plain English—right now—I'm hanging up.''

''You'll know me when you see me. What I want is for you to set fire to a house for me.''

''Not interested,'' Tilt said.

''Sure you are. I told you, I'll pay a fair price.''

''Not interested,'' he repeated, determined not to be. This could only be bad, bad news.

''Tilton, listen. If you don't help me out on this, I'll go to the cops with what I saw this morning. I'll turn you in.''

Shutting his eyes, Tilt pressed them into his face with thumb and forefinger. ''Okay, then, you listen. I'll meet you somewhere and hear what you have to say, but I'm not promising anything. I'm not admitting anything.''

''Fair enough. Let's make it the library bridge at one o'clock. You know where I mean?''

''Yeah, yeah.'' Tilton slammed down the receiver. Blackmail. Son of a bitch, he was being blackmailed.

■

''Where does Celia Vogle live?'' Maxey asked as she and Bailey Marker returned to the front yard of the

Gunderloy house. Clouds had crowded in front of the sun, temporarily darkening the scene.

"The brick Craftsman, two doors east of me."

Maxey saw the one he meant. The front door was propped open with a dinette chair, and two maroon throw rugs draped the porch railing. While Maxey was looking, Celia bustled outside, her arms full of a robust rubber plant. Setting the plant where it would get sun if the sun came back, Celia dusted her hands and, spotting Bailey, waved.

"Guess I'll go say hello," Maxey said, just having decided to. "Thank you for the tour. Maybe sometime I can see the inside."

"Maybe," Bailey said without any enthusiasm that could be misinterpreted as an offer to help.

Celia had disappeared into the house again by the time Maxey reached hailing distance. If Madame Gunderloy's mansion was a fanciful castle from a fairy tale, Celia's residence was the frog prince. It squatted in its shrubs, four-square and sturdy, all its blinds half-shut.

"Hello, Celia?" Maxey called, having mounted the steps and walked to the gaping portal without challenge.

Just inside on the left was a fieldstone fireplace big enough to roast an ox, and on the right a living room that stretched into dining room, the combined space like a ballroom with furniture. Footsteps creaked the gleaming oakplank floor, and Celia appeared at the far end of the dining room, wiping her hands on a tea towel. Her expectant smile was in place before she recognized Maxey.

"Well, hello. Come in. Checking out Fionna Estelle's pad, are you?" She yanked open a door and shouted, "Chet! Come down here. There's someone I want you to meet."

"I don't mean to bother you. You look busy," Maxey said.

"Oh, I'm good at appearing that way. So what do you think of the Gunderloy?"

"It's a great old house. I don't know anything about architecture, but I know what I like."

"Well, that's me, too. I don't care how gorgeous a condominium they've got designed to go on that lot, it won't have the individuality, the presence, of the antique that's there now." Celia backed up to yell once again for Chet.

"Did you attend the fire last night?" Maxey asked.

"Oh, yeah, wasn't that something? We'd got home from the dog races just a little before that. No sooner gone to sleep than sirens were waking me up. I've been logy all day."

Thumping and shuffling echoed from the stairwell. The man who appeared was smaller and older than Celia, his sparse hair made sparser by a military cut.

"I was on the phone," he explained as he crossed the room to them. He openly studied Maxey, his expression that of a school principal intending to disapprove whatever was on this new student's mind.

"Maxey, this is Chet. Chet, Maxey owns that little weekly paper. You know, the *Blatant Regard.*"

Maxey offered her hand. Chet had to transfer the book he carried—*Haunted* something or other—into his left hand, and he made a production of marking his place with that forefinger. When he did clasp hands with Maxey, he stared into her eyes. The cliché *cold fish* came into her mind.

Determined to be as sociable as Chet was aloof, Maxey beamed and said, "Your wife has been educating me on the Gunderloy place."

"My wife." He blinked and looked confused.

"Sister," Celia corrected.

"Oh, sorry. Wrong conclusion." But a natural one, Maxey thought, mildly annoyed with Celia for the sloppy introduction.

"Chet's on the faculty at CU," Celia embellished now. "English Department. Specializing in science fiction and dark fantasy."

Maxey had never been able to work a genre-fiction elective into her college schedule. "Cushy" was her admittedly unsupported view of a class where you were required to read what you wanted to read anyway.

"Lucky you, to have a fun job."

Chet ejaculated one short, decidedly nasty guffaw.

Well it was a dumb remark, the kind of thing one

of Reece's bimbos would say. Flustered, Maxey stepped closer to a painting on the wall beside her shoulder, prepared to admire it, whatever it was. Surprise flustered her all over again. A bare-chested man and an almost bare-chested woman strained together in what appeared to be a bed of roses. It couldn't have been comfortable—think of the thorns!—but the two seemed to be enjoying it.

"Wow," Maxey said.

Celia waved toward another frame farther along the wall. Same artist, same subject, except these lovers were in a pond full of water lilies. There were a dozen similar paintings trooping around the living room, Maxey now realized.

"I have a fun job, too," Celia said.

"You painted these?"

"They're paperback romance covers. I've got these young, gorgeous models in here all the time."

Maxey laughed. "How awful for you." She swung around to look at Celia and her brother.

If Celia ever switched to designing covers for the kinds of books that were Chet's specialty, she could use him and his scowling face for a model.

■

Tilt loitered on the pedestrian bridge that straddled Boulder Creek between the old and the new public library buildings. He didn't want to be here, and he felt like a standing duck. The bridge was busy with foot and bicycle traffic, mostly students wearing backpacks and preoccupied expressions. Nobody looked at Tilt.

Determined not to appear anxious to the one person who might be watching him, Tilt turned around and, elbows on the railing, stared down into the tobacco brown water.

He tried to pass the time by thinking who could have phoned. It took maybe one minute for him to inventory the meager possibilities and give up. He couldn't place the voice.

Okay, it didn't matter who. The thing was, could Tilt bring himself to torch a building because someone else wanted it done? Every fire he'd ever set had been strictly for his own pleasure, never for monetary gain. Arson for profit—that just didn't sound right.

A fat, cold raindrop splattered the back of his neck, and wet polka dots began to speckle the wooden railing. His watch said the guy was ten minutes late. Anger roiling his stomach, Tilt leaned out to spit into the creek. He flipped his shirt collar as high as it would go. The adjustment didn't make him feel any less vulnerable.

■

As soon as the *Regard* woman left, Chet Vogle had retreated upstairs again. Now he watched the skylight bead with rain and planned how he would kill his department chairman. In the kitchen below, Celia was cooking something involving tomatoes and onions, the scent headier than any expensive perfume.

He sat forward and fanned out a dozen books on his desktop. Of all the horrific covers—razor-toothed women, rat-ridden men, children with rattlesnake eyes—none depicted a fate bad enough for Dr. Leland Pharr.

Involuntarily, Chet relived the moment in Pharr's office when "the possibility" first raised its ugly head. "I think you should know," the old Pharr had said, "there's a strong likelihood we won't be renewing your contract in the fall."

No easing gently into the subject, no apologetic smile, not even a regretful shake of the head. Just, bam, you're going to be canned.

One year away from tenure.

"I thought we were going to augment the English faculty." Chet had tried to keep his voice level. "We've been turning students away, especially in the graduate courses."

"English lit. We're beefing up the classics."

"Well, I'm capable of that. I can teach Chaucer or Coleridge or whatever the hell needs teaching."

Pharr's head had begun shaking ten words ago. "We've got other people lined up—experts in the field." And then he'd droned on about the credentials of these wunderkind as if he expected Chet to applaud and marvel at the department's great good fortune.

Pharr had always liked flatterers, yes-men, and especially yes-women. Someone like Chet, who plodded along minding his own business and doing his fair share, went totally unappreciated.

A smack of thunder rattled the skylight glass, rousing Chet to the present. He lifted one of the paperbacks to study the flame-throwing dragon that loomed above an idealized female and her anatomically incorrect cohort. Only the fire was rendered with realism.

Chet's anger smoldered and flared. How would it feel to face the light and heat of a real, out-of-control fire?

However, revenge should fit the crime. Do unto others what they have done to you.

Chet pictured Leland Pharr flailing and screeching, impaled by a giant screw.

6

■ ■ ■

This time, the telephone rang while Tilt was in the kitchen snapping the tab off a Coors. His mother was gone. She'd taken the car and a grocery list and a verbal swipe at Tilt for not asking what she needed when he went out earlier.

The vaguely familiar voice said, ''Sorry I didn't make it. Something came up.''

''That's great by me, because I didn't make it, either,'' Tilt lied, and then he wondered if this was some kind of test. ''I got no interest in anything you have to say. I'm hanging up. Don't call back.''

''Wait!''

''You got nothing on me. But if you lay out some deal where I'm supposed to do a job for you, then I'll have something on you.''

The voice came back higher, whiny. ''We'd have something on each other.''

''Why the hell don't you set your own goddamn fire?''

There was a brief crackle on the line, a laugh perhaps. ''I'm afraid to, tell you the truth. It's dangerous work, isn't it?''

''For a lot more reasons than one,'' Tilt said, then disconnected the line. He chugalugged the beer and went to get another.

■

Maxey hitched her tan leather bag onto her left shoulder and braced the laundry basket against her right hip. She slammed the car door and crossed the street. Mrs. Waterford, wearing a faded blue plaid dress, white socks and white tennis shoes, and a pair of canvas gloves with kelly green thumbs, was weeding the flaccid-petaled petunias by the porch.

''That little rain shower was just right for this job,'' Mrs. W. said. ''Softened the dirt, so the roots and all yank right out.'' She held aloft a johnson-grass trophy.

''Think it's over?'' Maxey said, squinting skyward.

''Oh, I hope so. Timmie is taking me to Chautauqua this evening for supper on the dining room porch and an all-Mozart concert. You know how leaky that auditorium is.''

''A barn that needs a new roof and new siding,'' Maxey agreed. ''How nice, an outing with your grandson.''

''We're celebrating your giving him a job. It was sweet of you to help him out that way.''

''Oh, he'll earn it. The wages aren't that great.''

''Money isn't the main thing. Some things are more important.'' The old lady rolled her lips in against her teeth, her pale eyes vacant with some sudden thought.

Maxey turned to the porch steps. ''You have a good time tonight. Remember, no alcoholic beverages are allowed inside.''

Mrs. W. crackled and bent to evict a dandelion.

■

''Mrs. Pharr and I are going to the Colorado Symphony tonight—all-Mozart program. Should be excellent.''

Chet Vogle stood in Dr. Pharr's oak- and vinyl-furnished office in the fine arts building—not having been invited to sit down. He'd decided to give the old gasbag one more chance to do what was right before Chet himself did something that was wrong. That the chairman was actually in his office on a Saturday afternoon had seemed an auspicious omen. But seeing Chet in the doorway had launched Pharr on a litany of what all he had to do, none of it germane to the firing of Professor Vogle.

''I have a conception for a new graduate class,'' Chet finally interrupted. He surreptitiously wiped his damp palms on the back pockets of his jeans. ''A field study of early nineteenth-century American writers. We'd expend an entire semester busing to the places they frequented: Walden Pond, the House of the Seven Gables, Twain's Mississippi.''

Pharr was frowning, but he always did that when he thought hard about something.

''We could offer a second semester of modern writers,'' Chet rushed on. ''Florida Keys for Hemingway. Perhaps Steve King would permit us inside the gates up there in Maine.'' He laughed to show this last remark was—probably—facetious.

Pharr's head began to move in the wrong direction, swaying back and forth. ''Too expensive—both in money and in time. Students couldn't afford what we'd need to charge, and they'd be putting their other credit hours on hold for an entire semester.''

''Utilize several teachers,'' Chet said, answering the easier of the two objections. ''Make it a portable college where students would be taking a full complement of classes. There'd be plenteous time on the bus—''

''Not this year. I'll keep it in mind.'' Pharr began leafing through papers on his desk, looking for the place where Chet had interrupted him.

Literally biting his tongue, Chet backed toward the door. Hand on knob, he said, ''Please consider it. I'd be delighted to work up a detailed proposal.''

Pharr pinched the bridge of his nose as if he had a headache. Sighing, he began to read.

Wanting to scream, Chet strode out into the hall and pelted downstairs to his car.

■

Waiting for Sam to make the first reassuring move wasn't working.

The first thing Maxey had done after setting down the laundry basket and skritching Moe's intricate ears was check the answering machine. There was nothing on it except the click of someone who had exercised the right to remain silent and hang up.

Was she going to mope around wishing for contact she could initiate herself? Was she a woman or a mouse? Yanking the receiver to her ear, she dialed.

Sam's terse "Leave your number and I'll get back to you" made her roll her eyes.

"It's Maxey here. Listen, the cops may have a tap on this phone, so we have to be careful what we say. I had a great time in *b-e-d* with you, and let's *s-c-r-e-w* again in the near future. Okay?"

She waited a beat, hoping he'd pick up on his end, that he'd laugh and promise to hustle right over. When this didn't happen, she hung up gently and switched on the TV.

■

Mrs. Waterford's backside was numb. The Chautauqua dining room's Rocky Mountain trout had been delicious, and starlight rather than rain had penetrated the faulty roof of the concert hall. The orchestra had done Mozart proud, right down to the blessedly brief encore, and only the unpadded theater seat had given any cause for complaint.

Now Timmie helped her up, and they let the crowd drain away past them to the exits. She patted his arm, glad he was in no hurry, since her stiff old joints made speed almost impossible.

"That was lovely, wasn't it?" she said after clearing her throat to jump-start her voice.

Timmie was perspiring. Mrs. Waterford had never minded the honest scent of a man's sweat. She snugged her white clutch purse against her bosom, the way she used to carry schoolbooks so many years ago, and nodded at an occasional familiar face as it drifted by.

Leaning on her grandson's arm, she unlocked her knees and shuffled up the slight incline toward the back exit. They emerged into the mild night, where crickets were playing their own particular classics. Already most of the concert crowd had disappeared down the hill to the street.

Breathing in the green scent of the afternoon's rain, Mrs. Waterford said, "I always thought it would be fun to rent a cottage here for a week in the summer."

"Mmm," Timmie said.

She laughed. "That's exactly the reaction your

grandfather gave me. No enthusiasm whatsoever. That's why we never did it."

Funny, she couldn't *see* John anymore. Of course, she knew what he looked like from the photograph on the mantel. But she couldn't recall him in his three-dimensional entirety. What she did remember was the feel of him—the bottlebrush mustache, the silky-haired skin stretched over the long bones of his arms, the heat of his body radiating out to welcome her into bed at night.

As if he could read her mind, Timmie stopped, hauled a handkerchief out of a back pocket, and blew his nose. She needed to do that, too, but she sniffed and straightened her back instead.

They continued down the sidewalk. Car motors starting in the distance were the only evidence that other people were still out and about.

"They could certainly use a few more lights along here," Mrs. Waterford grumbled, sliding her shoes on the gritty pavement, feeling for steps down to the sidewalk. The overhanging trees shivered in their damp leaves.

Timmie helped her down the shallow steps and on across the street.

"Did we park uphill or down?" she asked, hoping it was the latter.

"You wait right here, Grandmother. I'll get the car."

"Oh well, I expect I could go with you and save the trouble," she said, but he had already gone.

How quickly everyone else had disappeared, eager to be home. A few minutes earlier, Baseline Road had been lined on both sides by parked vehicles. Now it was just a narrow street coasting down off Flagstaff Mountain into the south end of Boulder. The fortieth parallel of the world on any map, and here she stood with her toes on it. A person didn't have to look at the stars to feel insignificant.

She hadn't noticed which way Timmie went to get the car. Now she recalled that her gallant grandson had let her out in front of the dining room when they arrived this evening, to save her a walk. Even standing was beginning to be a problem, and she worried that he'd had to go so far to get the car, he'd find her sitting on the curb when he finally came back. But no, there was a bench over there. She looked up and down Baseline again, to see if her wait would be worth the walk to the bench.

With relief, she spotted a vehicle coming downhill. Good thing there wasn't any other traffic, because he'd forgotten to turn on the headlights.

It would feel good to crawl into bed. First, though, she'd stop in the kitchen for a small glass of iced tea and two of the chocolate chip cookies she'd baked that morning.

The approaching car was gathering speed, and she could see that it was the wrong shape and much too big to be her two-door Ford. No, Timmie wouldn't drive that fast, at least not while she was watching. She tightened her purse against her chest, mildly apprehensive, thinking of muggers.

To the east, a distant red stoplight flickered on and off, the illusion caused by swaying branches between here and there. Mrs. Waterford turned to look west again and took a startled step backward. The automobile, still without lights, had quietly grown larger. It was definitely going too fast, and now it was on the wrong side of the street.

She'd never be able to read the license plate number as it passed, but, by golly, she'd certainly try. Darn drunks on the highway these days. Torn between wanting to retreat to safety and wanting to lean forward to see the plate, Mrs. Waterford swayed in place.

Too late, she began to panic, to turn to move one foot to throw her weight away from the looming presence. She dropped the purse, groping air behind her, and suddenly Timmie was beside her somewhere, though she couldn't see him.

She hadn't heard Timmie scream like that since he was a toddler.

Her hand reached out for him and her mind was already lifting him up to her hug and the selfish-selfless comfort a mother never forgets how to dispense, and she didn't feel the bumper break both her legs below the knee and rip her feet from the still-tied black Trotter's oxfords and the hood push her down and under like grass being swept into the blade and her best navy dress being wound against the axle and not tearing but binding her fast to the undercarriage and more bones bending the wrong way until they broke and the sidewalk bursting her head and blood leaving a slug trail over the bench that didn't stop her and up to the lamppost that did stop her and the VW bus and even knocked them back several feet.

And she didn't feel any of that, because in real life things don't happen in slow motion; they happen too fast to appreciate or to comprehend or to change.

■

Maxey's head snapped up from the left-listing doze that the late-night movie had induced. Moe shared her couch, his warm weight draped across her shins, his snores as insistent as the current commercial's car salesman. Before she could slide into sleep again, the telephone shrilled.

Batting her eyes open, Maxey continued to sprawl in groggy indifference, listening as her answering machine fielded the call.

"Maxey, pick up if you're there," Sam's voice said, and she dived to obey, dumping Moe and then having to two-step around his indignant stance to reach the phone.

''Hi. How's BPD's finest?'' she said, smiling and ready to agree with whatever he suggested.

''Max. Honey—'' He huffed out a hard sigh, and Maxey's heart performed a jiggle-dip of apprehension.

Whatever he was about to say, she guessed that Sam hated to do it and that she was going to hate hearing it even more.

''Maxey, how about hopping in your car and coming over to Boulder Community to give us a hand here?''

''Sure.'' She felt a rush of relief that this request seemed to have no Dear John implications. ''What's up?''

''We've had another runaway vehicle. This time, it hit somebody.''

''Oh no!''

''Somebody you know—Mrs. Waterford.''

''Oh, Sam.''

''Her grandson, too, but he's not as bad.''

''I'm coming,'' she said, groping under the couch for her shoes.

''Drive slow and safe,'' he commanded just before she hung up on him.

■

Sam met her at the front desk and led her through the hushed building and up one flight of stairs, answering her questions in the low tones that befit a hospital and horrific events.

"Timothy's got a broken wrist. He's okay otherwise. Physically, that is. Mentally, he's a mess. Blames himself for not being quick enough to shove her out of the way or whatever."

"And so how bad is Mrs. Waterford?"

"Dead on arrival."

Maxey skidded to a halt. Sam gripped her elbow and urged her on.

He said, "This time, it was an old VW bus. Rolled from the owner's driveway about two blocks up Baseline."

"Anyone see someone fooling with it?"

"Nobody we've questioned yet."

"It was parked in a driveway?"

"Yeah."

"It had to be pushed out into the street?"

"Seems as though."

"Damn it, Sam."

"Yeah."

They came to the island of a nurses' station, and Sam stopped, reaching out to draw Maxey forward under his right arm as he drew someone else toward her under his left. "Maxey Burnell, Paula Koski," he said as Maxey came face-to-face with the cute little blonde from Pearl Street.

"Paula is my newest colleague. Joined the department a week ago,'' Sam said. ''We drew the call tonight on the Baseline accident.''

''Colleague,'' Maxey said, feeling frowzy, thinking that Paula's black minidress couldn't be called ''plainclothes'' by any stretch of the imagination. It had rhinestone buttons and a neckline that had nothing to do with her neck.

''Hi, Maxey,'' Paula said, gracefully offering her slender, ringless hand. ''Sam's told me so much about you.''

That was a lie, of course, a polite conversational cliché. Sam wasn't a talker. He didn't talk about Maxey even to Maxey.

''Timothy Waterford's in here,'' he said now, indicating a door opposite the station. ''What we'd like you to do is listen to him. Calm him down enough to get his story before the doctor gives him a sedative.''

Maxey planted her feet, suspicious that she was being conned in more ways than one. ''He knows his grandmother died? You aren't asking me to break the news?''

''He knows.''

Sam was dressed up, too, in a pale blue sports jacket Maxey had never seen before. When he reached in front of her to open the door, she caught a faint whiff of beer.

''You don't usually drink on duty,'' Maxey muttered into his shirtfront.

"Who says I've been doing my duty?" Sam muttered back.

Wishing she hadn't uncovered this much information, Maxey slipped from under his arm and into the room. Immediately, her jealousy scattered in the rush of sympathy she felt for Timothy, who lay on top of the farther of two beds, fully clothed, curled in on himself. His left forearm and most of his hand were encased in cream-colored fiberglass, or whatever the hell casts are made of nowadays.

Halfway across the floor, Maxey heard the door close. Perching on the edge of the high, taut-sheeted bed, she put her hand on Timothy's good arm. Without opening his eyes, he snarled, "I did it. I killed her."

"No, you didn't," Maxey said. She massaged his shoulders, trying to soothe some sense into him.

"It was all my idea. Supper and a concert. Park the car on Tenth. If we'd left the auditorium three minutes sooner, just *two* minutes even—"

"Don't." She hoped a brusque practicality was the right approach to take. "If you want to look at it that way, blame the symphony for playing an encore or the city for building Chautauqua Park on the side of a hill."

Timothy began to sob in earnest.

Through the window, Maxey could see a slice of night sky and another wing of the hospital paralleling this one. Over there behind those windows, other people suffered other pains. She focused her eyes and her mind on the clean black and sparkle of the sky until Timothy straightened up.

"We've got to get them, Maxey."

"Bet on it." As soon as she said it, she felt the promise root itself in her will, more tenacious than the johnsongrass in Mrs. Waterford's flower bed.

7

■ ■ ■

"We had just crossed the street seconds before," Leland Pharr said to Officer Martinez, who stood taking the report by the gaudy glow of emergency flares. "My wife had a pebble in her shoe, and we stopped on the way down Tenth to our automobile. A moment sooner, we might have been the ones hit."

"Did you see the accident happen?"

Knots of onlookers were beginning to unravel and drift away, everyone still speculating on the tragedy and thinking about whom to tell first.

"Oh yes. We were right there, Mrs. Pharr and I. We'd just started down Tenth Street, where we'd parked the Seville, and the screaming made us stop and turn around, and what a sight. What a sight."

"What, exactly, did you see?"

"Why, all of it. The van running over those poor people."

"You saw it hit them?"

"Yes, we did. We'll never forget it."

Mrs. Pharr, used to letting her husband do all the talking, nodded and nodded, her lips in a pinched line.

"Did either of you see anyone in the VW?"

"Oh, no, I don't think so. Did you, Joslynn?"

Her nodding circled around to become a negative shaking.

"Well, there couldn't have been," Dr. Pharr decided. "We would have seen them get out. Because we were only half a block away, and we rushed right back up there as soon as the thing happened. Didn't we, Joslynn?"

Martinez frowned at his mostly blank memo page. "Did you witness anybody on the street? Farther up the hill, say?"

"There could have been someone up there," Dr. Pharr allowed. "But all we saw was, in the words of John Milton, 'darkness visible.' "

■

Maxey slid into a booth in the hospital cafeteria and Paula scooted in on the opposite side. If this was a test of Sam's loyalty, he passed with flying colors, hauling out a straight chair from another table, setting it at the end of their table, and straddling it.

Maxey stirred her black coffee, her cheek propped on her fist. "He told her he'd get the car, which they'd parked on Tenth. Started to leave her standing there, on the north side of Baseline. But something—

he can't say what exactly—made him think something wasn't right. So he backtracked far enough to check on her. She was fine, just standing there, and then he looked in the other direction, west, and there was this . . . shape—coming toward them. No motor noise. No lights. Now he was really alarmed, remembering the runaway I almost tangled with a few nights ago. He ran back toward his grandmother but was too late to push her out of the way. The VW clipped him, spun him around, and he fell wrong on his arm. By then, it'd run over Mrs. Waterford."

Maxey swallowed too-hot coffee and blamed it for her stinging eyes.

"You taking him home tonight?" Sam asked, staring into his own coffee cup.

"No. The hospital wants to keep him overnight for observation. He's sleeping off a sedative right now."

Paula ran the splayed fingers of both hands through her hair, front to back, and it all fell into perfect place again, like water closing over the wake of a boat.

"So," Maxey said, "how did you two happen to catch this call? Dressed so nicely and all."

"We were at the concert," Paula said. "No off-duty for the wicked."

"On pickpocket patrol," Sam amplified.

"Sam's the best when it comes to undercover work," Maxey said, baring her teeth at Paula. Immediately ashamed of herself, she rushed to ask, "Where were you when the VW cut loose?"

"Long gone. Almost downtown," Sam said, pursing his lips to sip coffee. "You never know what to expect. You just never know."

■

"I know exactly what you're thinking." Chet swayed over Celia, who sat on the brown tweed sofa, her legs tucked under her red flannel robe, *The Color Purple* lying open on her lap. "You're rancorous because here I am staggering home way past midnight, my eyes at half-mast and my breath flammable."

Celia lifted the book and began to read doggedly.

Chet collapsed at the other end of the sofa, making the cushions wheeze. "I'm pissed, and so are you." His laugh sounded like the cushions.

"It's worth it to have you in such a good humor," Celia said without looking up. "You've been a holy badger lately."

"You'd have been a holy badger, too, if you were in my straits." Chet tried to prop his chin on his hand and missed.

Celia closed the book on her forefinger. "What straits? Why don't you ever share your problems with—"

"Sacked. Screwed and sacked."

"You lost your faculty post?"

He nodded, the tears welling up, ready to shame him further.

"Is that all?"

"What do you mean 'all'? My God, isn't losing my job enough?"

"You aren't sick? I was imagining you with some horrible terminal disease that you couldn't bear to talk about."

"This is terminal! I'm terminated. I'm dead as far as Pharr's concerned. All the good squeezed out of me. Too old."

"You aren't too old. You'll find another teaching position."

"Somewhere off," Chet keened. "Somewhere dull and unbeauteous. I don't want to move."

Celia shifted impatiently. "You don't have to move. You don't even have to get a new position. Our trust fund and the money I make from painting will keep us very nicely. You can write a novel like you've always want—"

"You don't know!" Chet's anguished cry hauled her up straight and made her cringe. "So just shut the fuck up and leave me the hell alone."

Five minutes later, after Chet had stumbled and slammed his way to his bedroom, Celia still sat, the book like a shield across her chest, amazed that this stranger had never shown his face before.

■

On Sunday morning, Maxey picked up Timothy at the hospital for the short ride home. She wished she'd thought to bring along some clothes for him. His white knees showed through holes in his suit pants, and the jacket draped over his shoulders had one sleeve missing and showed stains that didn't bear thinking about. He held the arm with its cast and sling out in front of him like a tennis player awaiting a serve.

They rode in silence except for Timothy's runny nose. He didn't have a handkerchief apparently, and Maxey, feeling each sniff as a jab to her nerves, didn't have a tissue to offer. Parking the Toyota in front of the house, she resisted the impulse to help as he struggled to unlatch the seat belt.

"She should have been coming home from church right now," Timothy said, shouldering the car door open and grunting as he pushed himself to his feet.

Maxey bit her lip against correcting him. Mrs. Waterford had never gone to church since Maxey had known her. Presumably, Timothy knew this as well as she, and his observation belonged in the category of aggrieved rhetorical remarks.

"Is there someone I can call for you?" Maxey asked, following him up the porch steps.

"It was just Grandmother and me." He unpocketed a key and jammed it into the front door lock.

"A friend? Someone to come stay with you for a while?"

"No," he said, pushing into the cool dimness of the living room. "I'll be okay."

Maxey hovered in the doorway for an uncomfortable moment. She had never been required to perform the role of sympathizer and helping hand before. Thank God.

"You want me to take you to the under—the funeral home?"

"Where's the car? Grandmother's Fairlane?"

"In the alley. The police brought it home."

"I can drive myself." He blotted his forehead with the one intact sleeve.

"Okay. But if you need anything . . ."

"I won't." He disappeared into the next room.

Feeling guilty but relieved—and guilty to be relieved—Maxey retreated to her own quarters.

She should have asked him if he wanted some lunch. On the other hand, she didn't want to be an oversolicitous pest. She hadn't had breakfast herself, and nothing that stared out at her from the refrigerator shelves inspired.

A fat, juicy hamburger—that's what she wanted. Gallons of iced tea, and French fries, the coffin nails of fast food. Why not eat like there's no tomorrow when that might be the actual case?

But not alone.

Thinking of Timothy, solitary and miserable in the room below her, she went to the telephone and dialed Sam's home number.

After four rings, the answering machine started up, and she quietly replaced the receiver. Changing her mind, she lifted it and dialed again, then listened to the end of the taped greeting.

"Hey, cop, pick up the phone. Come on, I know you're there, because you sure don't go to worship services Sunday mornings."

As the seconds ticked by, she felt the disappointment spreading like a dull toothache. She hung up.

Moe lay on the floor in a streak of sunlight, on his back, with all four legs up, a fat cat in every sense of the term.

"You must have been a saint in your last life to get to come back like this," Maxey said, bending to stroke his tummy. One of his eyes opened, and drifted shut again. "I'm going to McDonald's. Can I bring you anything? No? Don't say I didn't offer."

Grabbing up her purse, Maxey descended the straight shoot of steep stairs into the dry heat.

■

At the first stoplight, Maxey turned north instead of south. Maybe Celia would like to have lunch with her. That's if Celia didn't feel obligated to prepare Sunday dinner for her dour brother.

Nebraska Street lay quiet and motionless, like a stage set with a foothill-painted backdrop. Maxey crossed the wrong way into the other lane and parked in front of Celia's house. Switching the ignition off, she peered at the Gunderloy mansion, across the street and half a block away. Even from this distance, she felt the presence of ghostly fallen doves, could almost see them lounging about the shadowed veranda, drinking Taos tea and telling ribald stories.

The house next door to the Gunderloy would have seemed a large house somewhere else, away from its imposing neighbor. A wood-frame two-story with a bay window full of stained-glass work, it reminded her of Reece's apartment house, mostly because of the steep white staircase climbing up its near side.

Maxey followed Celia's pitted gray concrete sidewalk to the stone porch, noticing that the oak-stained front door was closed, wondering if this meant no one would answer her ring. She waited, rang a second time, and felt the twinge of disappointment that would precede a full-fledged case of the blues. Then the door whipped open and a naked man filled the portal.

She felt her jaw go lax as all that muscled, golden flesh filled her vision—shoulders, chest, arms, waist, stomach. On second look, the guy was not totally bare. He did sport the briefest of swimming briefs—white, to match the teeth he flashed in welcome.

"Help you, ma'am?"

"Celia?" she managed to inquire.

"Just a sec." His long blond hair floated away from his face when he tipped it to bellow at the ceiling. "Celie? Company."

As a butler, he needed a bit more training. Still, Maxey imagined most prospective mistresses would gladly overlook his inadequacies in favor of his more than adequacies.

From forehead to toes, his body shone like a basted turkey.

The padding of bare feet behind him made him turn, and he motioned with exaggerated impatience to Celia, who ducked her head to look at Maxey beneath his arm. Maxey felt relieved that, except for shoes, Celia was fully dressed in jeans and a loose man-tailored white shirt smudged with variegated paint.

"Hey, Maxey. Whatcha up to?"

"What are *you* up to?"

"Oh, this is just Brent. Brent Delaney, Maxey Burnell. Brent models for me, for my book covers. Monica and Gary are here, too. Come in, come in." Leading off across the oversized living room-dining room, Celia raised her voice to say across her shoulder, "They all have real jobs, so we have to work the modeling in on weekends and nights, most times."

Maxey followed her through another big room, a kitchen lined with oak cabinets and hanging copperware. Bringing up the rear, Brent swept a handful of carrot sticks off the butcher-block table and began to chew noisily.

"Watch your step," Celia said, jogging down

three of them to a sunroom that overlooked the verdant backyard.

An easel dominated the center of the floor. Propped on it, an oil painting in splashy reds and greens depicted Brent in all his muscular glory. The raven-haired woman draped over his arm showed as much creamy skin below as above her disheveled dress. Her pained expression might be embarrassment at Brent's presumptuous hand on her thigh, or it might reflect fear of being trampled by the white horse behind them, whose mane was nearly as long and flowing as Brent's.

''Does it make you hot?'' a little-girl voice asked, and Maxey found herself confronted by the painted lady's spitting image. Even the scarlet dress was hiked up and tucked around the waist to expose shapely legs. ''It sure makes me hot,'' she complained, fanning at her neck with a folded section of newspaper. ''Velveteen, yuck.''

''Maxey, this is Monica, and that's Gary,'' Celia said, pointing at another husky young man sprawled on a chintz-cushioned wicker lounge. She picked up a long-handled brush and a palette pimpled with paints. ''Gary is kibitzing today.''

''No I'm not. I'm the horse.'' Gary tossed back his head and fluffed at his conventional haircut. Monica swatted his foot with the newspaper.

''Places, everyone,'' Celia said.

Tossing aside the paper, Monica yanked Brent

around to face her, slapped his hand in place against her leg, and turned on an expression of avid desire. With his other hand, Brent jammed the last of the carrots into his mouth and chewed, every muscle in his face expanding and contracting. Before swallowing, he opened his mouth at Monica, and she rewarded him with a disgusted "Yuck," though her expression never changed.

Celia brushed silver highlights into the heroine's cleavage. "Have a seat, Maxey. What do you want to talk about?"

"Well, I really came to see if you'd go to lunch with me. But obviously, you're busy now."

"No problem. Give us fifteen minutes and then have lunch here with us."

"Oh, I hate to— Thanks, I will." Maxey crossed the sunny floor and sat in the wicker chair at right angles to Gary.

He hitched up straighter, turning toward her to be polite, and she saw that he was not as young as she'd thought. Tiny lines around his eyes and mouth, the embryos of wrinkles, branded him as at least, oh, thirty-five. He grinned at Maxey, and all the lines deepened in place, marks of his frequent good humor.

"I thought artists needed north light," Maxey said, gazing out at the quarter acre of bushes and trees in Celia's south yard.

"That's artists with a big *A*. I'm an artist with a

little *a.* If you don't hold still, Brent, I'm coming over there and nail your piggies to the floor."

"Oooo, kinky." He pinched Monica's thigh, making her squirm, too.

"If I was a big-*A* artist, I could afford professional models instead of spoiled brats." Celia continued to paint, ignoring her models as their erotic pose disintegrated into an arm-wrestling match.

Maxey doubted that Celia really needed the couple at this late stage. "What do you do for a real job, Gary?"

"Sell real estate. Monica and I both do. Adonis there works for a landscaping architect, but he's going to CU in prelaw."

Maxey pictured Brent straining the seams of a gray suit, summing up his case for the jury, charming socks and panty hose off right and left.

"Speaking of real estate, is there anything new on the Gunderloy house, Celia?"

"I'm still gathering petitions. The owner is still incommunicado. Skye and Skye are still blithering idiots."

"What's the zoning around here?" Gary asked.

"Great question," Maxey said. "Can developers actually build condominiums on this street?"

"We're residential two. That's single and multiple dwellings. Nothing over three stories, though."

"Oh, yeah. I noticed the place next to the Gunderloy looks like it has at least one apartment."

''McChristian's,'' Celia said, frowning at her work. ''They're in Italy on sabbatical. They ought to be here helping fight off the Skye boys. Okay.'' She put down the palette and brush. ''Finished.''

''Great,'' Brent said. He bowed low to Monica. ''May I have this dance, my delicate little kumquat?''

Before she could say no, he broke into a stomping, circling war chant. Maxey gasped as, at the height of his frenzy, he grabbed the top of his head and ripped off his leonine hair. Underneath, the real thing was reddish brown and cropped as close as peach fuzz.

When Monica, too, pulled off the cascade of red hair to reveal a cap of short red hair, Maxey couldn't help looking speculatively at Gary.

''This is mine. I am not bald under here,'' he said, yanking a tuft of dark brown hair on end.

Maxey followed Celia into the kitchen, laughing as she asked, ''What does Chet think of your business associates?''

''As little as possible. I'm afraid Chet doesn't have much patience or sense of humor, and Brent, especially, requires both.'' Celia washed her hands at the stainless steel sink and opened a cupboard to take down plates.

''What may I do to help?''

''Well, you want to take a page of petitions for your neighbors to sign?'' Grinning, Celia lifted a head of lettuce from the butcher-block table. ''Tear this up for salad.''

''What would you be doing with your time if you weren't so busy with the Gunderloy?'' The lettuce leaves scattered cool water as they snapped in her fingers, and Maxey suddenly felt ravenous.

Celia shrugged, but Gary, strolling in to watch them, said, ''She'd be visiting a nursing home or organizing a homeless shelter or some goody-two-shoes thing. Celia's a bitchin' good volunteer. Everybody loves Celia.'' To emphasize his statement, Gary skirted the table to hammerlock his hostess around the neck and rap lightly on her forehead.

Elbowing him away, Celia smacked the stack of plates against his midsection. ''Set the dining room table for five. That's all the fingers on one hand, to you.''

''Am I on overtime yet?'' Gary unerringly located the silverware drawer, rattled flatware onto the top plate, and walked away, balancing the load on one palm above his shoulder.

Brent made an entrance, buttoning a pink plaid shirt and stuffing it into the waist of his as-yet-unzipped jeans. Monica hurried around him, a cloth bundle under her arm, apparently on her way to a more private spot to dress.

''Hey, this would make an interesting feature in the *Regard*,'' Maxey said. ''Realtors and lawyers who double as romance heroes and heroines. And the artist who performs the magic. How about an interview, Brent?''

''Oh-ho-ho. Fabio, eat your heart out.''

Lunch was cold chicken sandwiches, tossed green salad, wedges of melon, and a Sara Lee cheesecake for dessert. Once, when the animated conversation and laughter coasted into momentary silence, a male cough sounded upstairs.

So much for Maxey's expectation that Celia would feel obliged to prepare brother Chet's meals.

8

When Maxey returned home, her answering machine was blinking. One message.

Sam's gruff command was simply, "Call me."

To show him she could still think for herself, Maxey first fed Moe, used the bathroom, and switched on the radio to KBCO. Then, Chris Rea's husky lyrics in the background, she settled into the couch and dialed Sam.

When he picked up, she panted and moaned into the receiver.

"Oh, hi, Max. Thanks for calling back."

"How'd you know it wasn't your new partner?"

"She groans a little higher, key of C."

Maxey laughed without enjoyment. "So you want to get together or what?"

"Can't. I'm on my way to the bureau. Just thought you'd like to hear the latest on the Waterford case."

"Oh. Yeah."

"We've got a couple suspects in interrogation."

"Hey, Sam, that's great. Who are they?"

"Kids. Like you thought. We got a break when a patrolman caught them in the act on Folsom Saturday night."

"No kidding? They pulled the same dumb stunt twice in one night? After killing someone?"

"They claim they had nothing to do with the VW on Baseline."

"Was there time? When did the patrolman bust them on Folsom?"

"Twelve-fifty-five. That's cutting it close, but they'd have had fifteen minutes to half an hour to hitch a ride or bus on up to Folsom. We just have to nail down the details."

"Uh-huh. How about if I come in and look at these two losers?"

"I thought you said you didn't see anybody the night the van made a pass at you."

"I didn't . . . I think. Maybe if I *see* these guys, I'll remember having seen them before."

"What, you planning to set them up?"

"No, flatfoot, I'm curious, that's all. It's the reporter in me."

That was his cue to say something about wanting to be the cop in her.

The line just breathed and crackled.

"Well?" Maxey said. "Okay if I come in? How long will you be there?" She half-expected him to change his story about having to work. This was the way good romances go bad.

"I'll call you," he said. "Maybe we'll get a confession and you won't need to come in."

Being tabled beat being voted down.

Maxey played two hands of solitaire, and then she drove to the police station.

■

The kid looked maybe fifteen, trying for twenty. He wore black jeans, black high-tops, a black T-shirt with an all-over design of white skulls, and one black hoop earring, left ear. Maxey guessed his hair would have been black had he not shaved it down to the quick. She watched him through the one-way glass as Sam went over the statement with him one more time.

"You folks should get yourself some help," the kid said, stretched out with only the nape of his neck and his tailbone touching the straight chair. "Hire somebody who understands the English language, so I don't have to keep repeating myself."

Sam leaned against the wall, arms folded, ankles crossed, jacket off and shoulder holster snug against his armpit. Maxey thought he looked sexy as all get out. He probably knew she thought so, too.

"Okay, Kirwin, so you were in the station wagon on Folsom Saturday night."

"I said so. Stewart and me. You got us red-handed."

"And an hour earlier, down on Baseline—"

"No way. Nope." He crossed his arms and stared at the tabletop in front of him.

"But you did the van on Sixteenth Street the night of May twenty-eighth?"

"Sure. If you say so."

"And the other van two nights before that?"

The boy nodded, mouth stiffened into a cocky grin.

"And the pickup . . . ?"

"Yeah, yeah, yeah. Listen, if I don't get a cigarette pretty soon, I'm going to run up that wall there."

"You did all these other vehicles. Why should I believe that you didn't do the VW bus on Baseline?"

"Because." He rocked the chair backward, let it drop, folded his hands behind his head, then unfolded them to jab one finger at Sam with each word. "I. Did. Not. Do. It."

"You saying it was Stewart who released the brake that time?"

Exhaling noisily, Kirwin drew himself up straight, the picture of frustration. "Oh, man—you deaf or what? We weren't in that part of town. I told you and told you."

"You think Stewart is going to keep on protecting the both of you? You think he isn't seriously thinking right now about turning prosecution witness to get out of serving any time himself?''

``Won't work, man. I know how you cops play your victims against each other. Stewart doesn't need to confess anything, because we didn't do anything.''

It was Sam's turn to exhale hard. He took one turn around the room before stopping beside the boy. Leaning over him, knuckles on the table, Sam said, ``Listen, Kirwin, I'm not censuring you. I've got sympathy for you. I know damn well you didn't mean to hurt anybody. It was an unfortunate accident. I want to help both you and Stewart.''

Kirwin gazed straight ahead, his eyes blank with boredom. ``Yeah? Yeah? Fuck you.''

Sam gave him a long, measuring stare. If he'd looked that way at Maxey, she'd have thrown herself on the mercy of the court. Kirwin, however, didn't even twitch.

Sam tossed a pack of cigarettes and a matchbook on the table and walked out. Moments later, he joined Maxey in the dim observation booth. Kirwin, having shaken out a cigarette, lit it, inhaled, blew out a smoke ring, and stuck his middle finger through it at the one-way window.

``What's the other kid like?'' Maxey asked as Sam sat on the folding chair beside hers.

``Younger. Scared.''

``And his story?''

``Same. They were out for laughs. Their own private demolition derby. Fun to see the smashup. Ckkrrshpow!"

"But they don't admit to Baseline."

"These kids may be short on good sense, but they aren't dumb." Sam rested his hand on her knee and massaged a circle.

"So what happens next?"

"Their parents will have them out on bond tomorrow. Hire attorneys."

"That isn't what I meant," Maxey said, putting her own hand considerably higher than Sam's knee.

Before she could massage, though, he trapped her hand and lifted it away. "I'm on duty, scoop."

■

The house seemed to be throbbing. Swimming up from a dream of nothing in particular, Maxey stared at the dim bedroom ceiling and waited to find out what had wakened her.

"Eee-yow!" a hoarse voice shouted.

She held her breath, stone-cold awake now.

Guitars squealed, and drums rattled like machine-gun fire.

Maxey threw off the sheet and scuffled the floor for her slippers. Fighting an inside-out sleeve, she hauled on her white terry robe as she hustled down the stairs. The stairwell pulsed with rock and roll at warp volume.

There was no use knocking at Timothy's door. It

was unlocked, and Maxey walked into the living room, where every lamp burned. The relentless noise felt like a high wind to be leaned into, every step hard fought. The kitchen lights all glared. The hall and every room along it glowed like a party without guests. Covering both ears, Maxey reached the far bedroom, launched herself at the stereo, and wrenched every knob counterclockwise till the howling stopped.

Blinking at the crash of sudden silence, she turned to look at Timothy, who lay flat on his back on the bed, fully clothed, his cast-encumbered wrist on his stomach and the other wrist over his eyes.

"If it's loud enough, I can't hear myself think," he said from under his arm.

"I wouldn't mind, but your other neighbors might. Is there anything I can do for you? Does your arm hurt?"

While Timothy didn't answer, Maxey looked around the little room. One bed, one kitchen chair beside one dressing table, one window with a pull-down blind and white lace curtains, one rag throw rug beside the bed. One young man with no one to love him.

Maxey felt sympathy clot her throat and determinedly cleared it away. "Hey, how about if I shut off all the lights as I go out, so you can afford next month's bill."

He lifted his arm off his face, blinking red, raw eyes at her. ''I'm afraid of the dark.''

''Oh. Well. Listen, Timothy, I don't know whether this will help or not, but the police have two kids they think are responsible for the joy-rolls.''

He squirmed into a sitting position. ''No shit? They think these kids killed my grandmother?''

''Maybe. There's no proof—''

''That's what I need—to know the jerks responsible are going to pay. So I can get on with my life.''

''Right, but don't get your hopes—''

''You got any sleeping pills?''

''No, but maybe aspirin would help you relax enough to sleep.''

''I don't need anything. Leave the lights on, though.'' He rolled onto his side, dismissing her with his broad back.

Maxey retreated through the house. It still smelled like Mrs. Waterford—like peaches and Ivory soap. Maybe that's why Maxey, crossing the living room, didn't think twice about lifting an antimacassar from the nearest chair and bearing it home with her.

■

On Monday morning, Maxey sat down at the kitchen table with warm toast in one hand and the telephone receiver in the other.

''Humm?'' Reece mumbled into her ear after five and a half rings.

"Do you know what time it is?"

"Honey, I don't even know what day it is."

"You need to go down and open the office. I've done it for the last hundred and seventy-eight consecutive days, so it's your turn." Maxey bit into the toast and enjoyed the decadence of butter oozing across her tongue.

"Why? Are you sick?" Reece asked.

"I have something to do before I come in."

"Ah. Ms. Mysterious. What's the matter? Nails taking too long to dry?"

"I'm writing a story about Mrs. Waterford getting killed by a runaway VW bus. I'm going to check out the scene of the crime."

The receiver rustled and clanked, and Maxey pictured Reece struggling to sit up, bumping the phone against the bed frame. "Your Mrs. Waterford? What a goddamn shame. What happened?"

"That's what I want to know. Sam's got a pair of badass teens on hold for it. I need to prove they did it, or someone else did."

"Sam put you on the payroll, did he?"

"It's a personal thing."

"Yeah, so's a heart attack, but that doesn't mean you should go looking for it."

"You just don't want to get up and open the office." She popped the last bite of bread into her mouth and licked the cholesterol off her fingers.

''Okay, Brenda Starr,'' he said with a sigh. ''I'll open.''

''Good. I'll see you later—Hank.''

■

Maxey took Broadway to Baseline and turned west toward the entrance to Chautauqua Park. Opposite the gray stone steps, she swooped the Toyota into a parking space, climbed out, and walked around to examine the nearest lamppost. It was creased three feet above the ground like a beer can squeezed by a giant hand, red-orange paint scarring the post's military green.

Maxey hiked up the street toward the Flatirons, past modest Victorian houses with apron lawns stitched by the roots of elderly trees. Across Baseline, in the meadow area of Chautauqua Park, a swarm of young men in shorts and little else kicked a soccer ball and insults back and forth. An occasional car bustled up or down the street, stirring the dusty air.

The sidewalk steepened. Maxey wished she'd asked Sam the address of the owner of the VW van. When she stopped to breathe and look back, Baseline fell away behind her like a black ski jump.

A screen door slapped as a woman scuffed out of the house Maxey was passing. The woman clothespinned a letter to a white mailbox on the shingled front wall. Turtlelike, her small sleek head nestled in the shell of her dowager hump.

"Hello," Maxey called. "Could you tell me which house is the one where the van rolled out of the driveway two nights ago? The one that had the accident?"

The woman gave no sign of hearing, fumbling with the clothespin, shuffling around to return the way she'd come. She labored to open the screen door and work her way inside. Maxey almost missed seeing the scrawny finger pointing straight across the street before the door smacked shut.

Chautauqua Park had given way to a row of eclectic residences. Maxey crossed over to the one indicated—a brick ranch with white trim and no distinguishing characteristics. The single-car garage yawned open, exposing the back end of a green sedan. Muffled sounds of someone working under the raised hood drew Maxey up the short driveway.

"Hello . . . excuse me?" she called, stopping in the shadow of the roof.

A large round head wearing yellow goggles swayed to see past the hood barrier. "Yeah?"

"May I ask you a question?"

"What about?"

"I believe it was your van that was stolen and wrecked on Saturday?" She smiled, tucking her hands into the back pockets of her jeans, going for the casual, harmless look.

The head jerked out of sight. The sedan rocked back and forth with whatever he was doing to it. "What's it to you? I already talked to the police and reporters and the insurance guy."

"I'm a friend of the family of the woman who was killed." Maxey stepped into the cool garage and lowered her voice accordingly. "I want to find out who did this to her."

The hood slammed shut, and the round brown face reappeared. Skimming the goggles off and parking them on top of his spongy black hair, the man looked Maxey over. Working a blue bandanna out of the rear pocket of his tan coveralls, he wiped his hands as he strolled forward. He had the face and physique of a bodyguard on the old *Hawaii Five-O* program.

"Her grandson—the one who was with her—he's taking it very hard," Maxey said.

"Want a beer?"

"No thanks. Not this early in the day."

He leaned against the side of his car. "Ask me, it was murder."

"Sure. A person takes another person's life, no matter how he does it—"

"Nah, that's not what I mean. Here, look." He stalked out into the sunlight. "The VW's parked here, facing the street, the way I always leave it. Doors unlocked. Safety brake on. You live on a hill like this, you always got to put the safety brake on, see what I mean? The ignition key's safe in my pocket in the rec room in the basement. I'm watching *Saturday Night Live.*

"So you didn't hear anyone. No unusual noises?"

"Right. First I knew, a cop's knocking on my front door, asking if this is my license plate number."

"And your wife or your children?"

He shook this off as if it was a dumb question. "I haven't got anybody right now. But look at this." He strode down to the edge of the street. "See, the guy lets off the brake, and he steers my bus out my drive, and then he aims it down there and hops out. You see anything funny about where it ended up?"

Obediently, Maxey studied the path the VW had taken, from point A, where she stood, to point B, her little white Toyota on the opposite side of the straight street. Baseline, already narrow, pinched down smaller wherever cars were parked.

Maxey said, "Well, it's hard to picture how that big a vehicle could have traveled that far without crashing into something else first."

"Exactly. You ask the police. There wasn't one scrape of orange paint on one parked car between here and there. What does that tell you?"

Maxey shook her head.

Impatient, he answered himself. "It was steered all the way." He nodded, mouth compressed into a knowing grin. "Steered all the way."

"Then where was the perp—this scumbag—when the bus hit Mrs. Waterford?"

"He jumped out somewhere along the line. Rode it down so far and then jumped and ran."

Maxey felt deflated. She'd been expecting to waste this man's time, and here he'd been wasting hers. "So you aren't saying he meant to kill Mrs. Waterford?"

"Maybe not the old lady. Could have been her grandson was the target. Could have been somebody else in the neighborhood was. The bus might not've gone where the killer expected after he jumped out."

"Have you told the police your theory?"

"Heck no. It's none of my business."

Maxey thought that his VW being the instrument of death made it very much his business. She smiled, preparatory to leaving him. "Thank you for talking—"

"Tell you something else." He leaned toward her, and the goggles on his hair winked twin suns into her eyes. "I worked and worked on that old bus's steering, but I never could get it fixed. Here's the thing. It always pulled to the right. Always." The man stepped back and folded his arms, chin high with triumph. "Think about that."

■

Tilt slid lower in the hard student desk and parked one ankle on the opposite knee. He usually sat at the front of the room, but today he had chosen a seat off to one side in the next to the last row.

The twenty-some students quieted from a murmur to a rustle as Professor Vogle gave them the evil eye over his lectern. Most instructors stopped taking attendance after the first few days. Vogle not only called the roll, he started before the bell, and two unexcused absences or three tardies reduced any final grade by a letter. Once, he had even made a big thing about a guy falling asleep during the lecture.

"Hammerberg."

"Present."

"Ives."

"Here."

"O'Meara."

"Here-a." The response was strictly habit, no longer drawing any titters from the audience or hard looks from Vogle.

Tilt chewed on his pencil, paying more attention than usual to this exercise in wasted time. As he'd paid more attention to everything and everyone for the last couple of days, trying to spot his wanna-be blackmailer.

"Tilton."

He almost forgot to answer. "Yo," he called, squirming up straighter in the seat.

Vogle, annoyed, erased at his roll book. "Waterford." Staring out over the top of his reading glasses, Vogle repeated it louder. "Waterford."

"Uh, I think he's at his grandma's funeral," a female voice chirped.

"Suuure, he is," a male one mocked, and everyone laughed.

"Well," Vogle said, snapping the book shut. "Genuine grandmothers do occasionally depart this world, just as little brothers, once in an azure moon, do put homework into fires."

Tilt bit too hard on the pencil and felt paint flake between his teeth. He wished he could make everyone in the room say *fire,* to see how many pronounced it *fi-yer* like Vogle and like Tilt's prospective blackmailer.

9

■ ■ ■

"You must be Maxey."

"Why must I? Is Michelle Pfeiffer taken?" Maxey hit the save key and swiveled her chair around to see who'd come into the office.

The man walking toward her made her wish she could take back the flippant remark. He wore an ivory silk shirt, slacks the color of slate, and black loafers that squeaked across the floor in an Italian accent. Not that money impressed Maxey. Still, it couldn't hurt to be polite.

"Hi. Help you?" she asked.

"I'm sure we can help each other."

Uh-oh. A salesman.

The toilet flushed in the rest room in the back corner, and Reece came strolling out, patting his hands dry with an industrial gray paper towel.

"I'd like to take out an ad in your paper," the man said, hauling out a side chair and settling into it as if it was upholstered and his.

"Great." Maxey reached for a scratch pad. "What kind of ad?"

"Standing, if we're all lucky."

"Hi, I'm Reece Macy," Reece interrupted, stretching to offer his clean and dry hand.

The man stood up long enough to clasp it. "Charles Skye."

Maxey was too busy running the name Skye through her mental database to feel slighted that she didn't get a handshake. "Skye and Skye? That Skye?"

"Yes, probably. It depends on which one you have in mind," he said, smiling easily, as if he'd done it all his life.

Thinning brown hair, tanned face, a paunch the size of a fanny pack—he must be in his forties and therefore the junior member of the development firm.

"Let's start with a full-page spread," he said, getting down to business. "Just our name and the words *For the life of your time.*"

"Nice slogan," Reece said.

"Oh, and the phone number, smaller and off in one corner. After we get folks' attention, we can start listing our services and achievements in the ads."

"Fine," Maxey said, trying to look as if strangers walked in off the street every day and laid easy revenues in her lap. "You'll want to see a display of our rates."

He waved this off, the ring on his little finger

winking its diamond eye. "I trust you to charge what's fair. Send me the bill." He buried the ring momentarily in a trouser pocket, pulling out a white-and-navy business card to pass over to Maxey.

Maxey wondered if Skye was too good to be true. Maybe his company needed *Regard* advertising because all the other area newspapers had shut them off for nonpayment.

"How did you hear about us?" she asked.

"Timothy Waterford. Aha, I see you're surprised. You don't know yet what a hotshot go-getter you've hired yourselves. He was in our building Saturday, canvassing for advertisers. Made you sound good. Maybe you'd give me an old copy of the paper so I can see what I've been missing."

Reece scrambled to fetch the request. "You want a cup of coffee, too?"

"No thanks. I have to move along. No rest for the self-employed." He rolled the *Regard* Reece found into a bat and held it aloft. "Okay if I keep this?"

"No! I don't believe it." The mall door clapped shut and Celia Vogle strode across the floor. "The slimy condo king himself, out among the commoners on Pearl Street Mall."

Charles Skye's easy smile stiffened into a grimace. "Ms. Vogle."

Celia's wind-mussed hair stood out on all sides as if her emotions had electrified it. Reece stared at her with the apprehension of a Hansel caught holding a chunk of her gingerbread house.

Maxey performed hasty introductions, which no one acknowledged. Celia continued to sputter and glare. Skye continued to edge toward the door. Reece continued to cringe.

"Send me a tear sheet so I can see how it looks, will you?" Skye called as he reached his goal and escaped into the sunshine. The door slammed on Maxey's answer.

"Maxey." Celia whirled around and gave her an accusing look. "You could use a good fumigator in here. What did he want? Oh, Maxey, are you interviewing him for your news story about the Gunderloy? You don't have to tell both sides, just the *right* side."

It wasn't any of Celia's business, but she would surely see the evidence in Thursday's paper, so Maxey answered. "He came in to buy some advertising. Now that you mention it, I should have gotten some quotes for the story."

"You do have the right to refuse anyone's business, you know."

Ignoring this invitation to debate Skye further, Maxey said brightly, "So what brings you to the *Regard*?"

Celia thumped her black patchwork handbag on the corner of Maxey's desk and withdrew a sheaf of papers. "I brought you this stuff about the

Gunderloy, to help you with your article. It's mostly historical information from library books.''

''That's great. Thanks.''

''You haven't found out who owns it, have you?''

''No. I thought I'd run over to the courthouse this afternoon.''

''Good. I should have done that, but I wasn't sure what department, and then what would I do with it once I had the owner's name?''

''Uh, call her the slimy queen of the condos?''

For a moment, Celia's jaw clamped down hard. Then she burst into her happy, full-out laugh. ''I scared the bastard, didn't I?''

''Celia, you need to learn to assert yourself more,'' Maxey said, laughing with her. ''Don't be so shy.''

By now, the drama apparently over, Reece sat at his desk, ripping open the mail with what had come to hand—a screwdriver. He raised his voice above their giggling. ''This article you're going to write about the Gunder-whatsit. You aren't going to jeopardize Skye's advertising with us, are you?''

Celia raised an eyebrow, waiting for Maxey's answer.

''When have we ever pulled any punches to avoid alienating advertisers or anyone else? The *Regard* has a reputation for rushing in where the *Daily Blahs* fear to tread.''

Now Celia raised a fist. ''Amen.''

"Ah nuts," Reece said.

After Celia left, reminding Maxey one more time to "call me" as the door swung closed between them, the office settled into a hush conducive to getting a little work done.

Maxey opened the computer file of the editorial she'd been writing before Skye's arrival. While the disk drive popped and hummed in search, she swiveled toward Reece. "Which county office can tell me who owns the Gunderloy?"

He sat at his desk and fed a blank paper into the maw of his typewriter. "I'd phone the assessor's office, ask who pays the tax on it."

"Brilliant." She reached for the Rolodex gold mine she'd inherited from Jim and paged through it. Repeating the number under her breath, she dialed. A busy signal bleated.

Scooting her chair into position, she finished her editorial chastising people who park in handicapped spaces when their only handicap is impaired consideration for others. This finished, she pushed the redial button on the phone and leaned back, watching Reece while it rang.

As he touch-typed, he frequently bent lower to read from his notes, then straightened again, frowning. Maxey bet herself that he needed glasses, but she also bet it would be a hot day in heaven when he admitted it.

"County assessor's. Could you hold?"

Before Maxey could say yea or nay, the line clicked and an instrumental "Stranger in Paradise" wafted into her ear. She glanced at her watch: 12:40. Bad time to call. This was confirmed when the music shut off in midswell and a second later a dial tone acted as encore. Maxey dropped the receiver into the cradle.

"I'm going to lunch."

Reece didn't answer, his attention fully engaged in trying to read his own handwriting.

Maxey turned left out the front door. She didn't stop at the Dilly Deli, thinking she could find the hot-dog vendor in the next block and then visit the courthouse in person. The brick walk, dappled with sun and shade, accommodated the usual unusual pedestrians, including a woman shopper wearing a sequined, low-cut purple gown but no shoes, and an apple-nosed clown on stilts.

Maxey found the hot-dog vendor at his regular spot, surrounded by customers who must, like Maxey, deliberately blank out thoughts of his ware's ingredients. She ordered hers plain except for mustard, and, juggling a Sprite in the other hand, she strolled east while she ate.

The courthouse lawn adjoining Pearl Street Mall spread festive as a picnic, littered with people enjoying the sun. Some ate from fast-food bags, some read newspapers or paperbacks, and some played guitars or Frisbee. The pale stone building sat in the midst of this activity like an immense Art Deco paperweight.

Maxey paused on the fringe of the grass to finish her sandwich. The sun weighed on her hair like a hot hand.

If she followed the sidewalk to the courthouse entrance, she would have to pass a gauntlet of panhandlers with their beards, gray clothes, and lackluster eyes. Deciding that she'd rather listen to a few more minutes of Muzak, Maxey crumpled her napkin, knocked back the last of the Sprite, threw both into the nearest trash barrel, and returned to the office.

Reece had done it again—hung the red-and-white plastic BACK AT ? O'CLOCK sign on the door and gone to lunch before she returned from hers. He hadn't even filled in the blank for what time the office would reopen. Maxey unclenched her teeth, unlocked the door, and whisked the sign inside. She could hardly wait for Timothy to begin helping out.

Of course, Timothy wouldn't be in this afternoon. Maxey pictured him spending the interminable day on his bed as the quiet house gathered dust and shadows.

This time when she dialed the assessor's office, a male voice answered promptly and pleasantly. She gave him the Gunderloy's address and asked for the owner's name and address.

"It'll take a couple minutes, ma'am. Want to hold?"

"Definitely."

Since help seemed on the way, she felt cheerful enough to hum along with one hundred violins playing a Beatles medley.

"Ma'am? You still there?"

She almost sang, Yeah, yeah, yeah. Instead, she said, "Did you find it?"

"Yep. Twenty-ten Nebraska Street. The property belongs to—let's see, you wanted the party's address, too."

"I don't have to have that yet if you didn't get—"

"No, I got it."

Papers rustled, and then Maxey heard her own address recited. She frowned at the barren scratch paper she had pulled into readiness.

"That's the owner's address," the man continued. "And the owner's name is Elizabeth Hadley, um, Waterford."

Maxey sucked in a disbelieving breath. Later, when she'd had time to recover from the surprise, she hoped she'd thanked the man who had sprung it on her.

When Reece ambled in, chewing on a toothpick, Maxey didn't break stride in the story she was typing about the threatened whorehouse. Of course, she couldn't actually finish it until she knew more about the Waterford connection.

She also couldn't telephone Celia as she'd promised she would do. It seemed disrespectful to discuss with a new friend the affairs of the dead landlady who'd also been her friend. Anyway, Maxey didn't have the information Celia wanted, which was who owned the Gunderloy *now.* Timothy had probably inherited everything from his grandmother, but it wasn't a certainty.

Could it really be only a coincidence that Timothy had talked to Charles Skye on Saturday? Was he in Skye's office on some business for his grandmother? Might Skye have had anything to do with Mrs. Waterford's dying that same night? If Maxey could find proof of that, Celia's jubilance would be impossible to bear.

Much as she dreaded the thought of it, Maxey would have to interview Timothy tonight.

But when she drove home at six, although the downstairs lights still glowed anemically in the late-afternoon sun, Timothy didn't seem to be home. When he didn't answer her knock at the closed front door, she tramped around to the rear of the building to make sure the Ford was gone, so that she could stop picturing Timothy collapsed on his bed, dying of an aspirin overdose. The little white garage, too small to store anything except one midsized car, sat empty as a cardboard carton, its two wooden flaps open.

Overhead, at Maxey's living room window, Moe paced the sill, yowling for her to quit goofing around and come feed him.

■

After soup and salad and a nap on the couch that she hadn't intended taking, Maxey telephoned Sam at home, bracing herself for the disappointment of his answering machine.

"Yeah, hello," grated in her ear.

"It's the real you all right."

"Hi, Max. What's up?"

"Have your boys confessed to Baseline yet?"

"Negative. They're home in their own cozy beds tonight."

"I talked to the guy who owned the VW bus."

"Valeros?"

"God, I'm slipping. I didn't even get his name."

"So what did you get? Propositioned? The guy looked like he could use a good woman. Or a bad one, even better."

"You're disgusting. Will you shut up and listen? He said it was murder."

"It's always murder when you need a woman."

"Sam, damn it."

"Okay, okay, sorry. The bus rolling downhill was murder."

"Yeah. Did he tell you his theory?"

"No. Wait a minute . . . I can't reach my beer." The receiver clinked, and a moment later, Sam said, "Go ahead."

"Valeros says his bus wouldn't have rolled that far

down Baseline in a straight line. The steering had a problem where it pulled to the right. So it should have veered that way before it got to Mrs. Waterford. Instead, it veered left and hit her. Sam, he thinks someone was in it, steering.''

''Then how come nobody saw this someone? How come Timothy, who was right there, didn't see the guy jump out and run?''

''Timothy was in shock. You could have unloaded an elephant from the front seat and he wouldn't have seen it.''

''How about the other witnesses? Dr. Parr or Pharr or whatever his name is.''

Maxey heard beer chugging down Sam's throat. ''Where was he? Driver's side or passenger's side of the bus?''

Sam belched gently. ''About twenty yards away, down the side street there—Tenth, I think. Driver's side, to answer your question. So he or his wife should have seen anyone in it.''

''The killer could have bailed out on the passenger's side and gotten away in the confusion.''

''You find him and ask him.''

Downstairs, a door slammed. Maxey stood up and carried the phone to the window to look into the backyard. Light streamed across the shrubbery from the Waterford kitchen windows. The garage doors had been closed.

''You want to rent a movie?'' Maxey asked, returning to the couch. ‘‘Bring your six-pack over here?’’

‘‘Better not. I think I’m catching cold.’’

‘‘Oh. I hope not.’’

‘‘You and me both. Talk to you next time.’’ The line disconnected.

Feeling a little sniffly herself, Maxey put on her tennis shoes and ran downstairs.

She pressed the front doorbell and stepped back to wait. The overhead porch light burst on, throwing her shadow on the closed door like a negative ghost. The door shuddered open and Timothy leaned into the intervening screen, making it crackle like ice about to shatter. His scrambled hair, stubbled jaw, and wrinkled black trousers reminded Maxey of the panhandlers at the courthouse.

‘‘Hi,’’ she said too brightly. ‘‘Can I come in?’’

‘‘May.’’ He smiled as if he had Novocain in his lips. ‘‘You may come in, if you can.’’

‘‘You don’t need to pass any more grammar tests,’’ she said, slipping past his outstretched arm pushing the screen open. ‘‘Did you eat yet?’’

Timothy led her toward the kitchen, reaching around the archway to the bedroom hall to switch on one more light. ‘‘Stopped for a pizza on my way home from the funeral parlor. The service is tomorrow afternoon.’’

‘‘I’m surprised you could schedule it that soon. But it’s good to get it over—’’

''No need to wait for out-of-town relatives.'' Timothy raised his voice, aggrieved. ''I'm it . . . the last of the Waterfords. The funeral director wanted to have what he called a viewing. He called it that even though the coffin will be closed. I don't want to sit around a funeral home for two, three hours staring at a closed box and listening to her friends talk about old times. What good would that do Grandmother?''

Dropping into a chair at the kitchen table, Timothy picked up a cup of what looked like coffee. He laughed and shook his head. ''Sounds like a novel—*The last of the Waterfords.* I've got to get myself a woman and an heir.''

''You and Mr. Valeros,'' Maxey said, opening two cupboards before she found the right one. She lifted down the least fragile-looking cup and spooned instant coffee into it.

''Who's that?'' Timothy said without much interest. Maxey saw this as an improvement over yesterday, when he wouldn't have responded at all.

''Timothy, I know how hard it is for you to talk about the accident, but if we're going to find the no-brainer responsible, I need to ask you some questions.''

''Sure. I understand. What do you want to know?''

She finished making her coffee. Sitting down opposite him, she watched his face. ''Timothy, do you know of anyone who might have wanted to hurt you? Maybe even kill you?''

Surprise erased the bleakness in his eyes. ''Me? Kill me? What kind of crazy question is that?''

''One slightly less crazy than the one about whether anyone could have wanted to murder your grandmother.''

Timothy's pain reappeared, his eyes glittering and his mouth pinched.

Maxey looked down into her cup as if it were the most interesting thing in the world. ''Sorry, Timothy. But it isn't as idiotic an idea as it first sounds.'' She forced herself to look at him. ''Did you know that Elizabeth owned some property in Boulder?''

''Uh, this house, of course. And a commercial building on East Arapahoe. Plus a place over on the west side.''

''The old Gunderloy house.''

''Yeah, that's right. She told you about that?''

''No, I just sort of found out. I don't know about the property on East Arapahoe, but the Gunderloy is pretty valuable, and it's a controversial historic building. You obviously know Charles Skye. He came to the office today to order some advertising. Way to go, Timothy.'' She smiled wider than necessary and waited for him to explain why he'd happened to be meeting with Skye on Saturday.

''I had to take some papers to him from Grandmother.''

''You don't know what they were?''

He shrugged. ''They were in an envelope.''

"Timothy, do you know whether she was going to sell the Gunderloy to Skye and Skye?"

"She didn't know herself."

"And now it will be up to you?"

"I guess." He stood up abruptly, as if he couldn't bear to sit still a moment longer. "Who else would she leave it to?"

"Did she make a will?"

"I never saw one. If she didn't, I get everything, right?"

"I guess."

"I won't say I don't need it." Timothy leaned against the counter. After a moment, he shifted to look hard at Maxey. "Why did you think someone might want to murder me?"

"I didn't. But there's something peculiar about the way the van rolled. It should have veered right, because of a chronic steering fault. Instead, it went left, toward you and your grandmother. So maybe someone was inside at the controls."

"Incredible. That's just so off-the-wall."

"So you can't think of someone who'd do that to you or your grandmother?"

He shook his head impatiently. "Maybe we weren't the ones meant to get hurt. Who else was around? How about Dr. Pharr and his wife? There are plenty of people who'd want to kill Pharr. Anybody who's ever taken one of his stupefying classes, for starters."

"Yes, but the Pharrs had left Baseline and were walking down the side street."

"Well, maybe this alleged hit person had bad timing and started the van down the hill too late. Maybe the professor walked too fast."

"You didn't see anyone else around."

"For the cazillionth time—no."

Maxey stood and rinsed her cup, gazing out the window at the sky, which had ripened into a plum black. When she turned to go, she caught Timothy staring at her ass, and she felt a swoop of relief. The boy was going to be all right.

10

■ ■ ■

On Tuesday, Maxey began her work at the office by telephoning Celia to tell her about the Waterford/Gunderloy connection.

"Hello," a male voice answered on the fifth ring.

"Hi. May I speak to Celia?" Maxey flicked on the computer to warm up while she talked.

"Not here. Who's this?"

"Chet? This is Maxey Burnell. You want to give her a message to call me?"

"When was the last time you saw her?"

It seemed like an odd question. "Uh, yesterday about noon. Here in the office. Why?"

"Did she indicate where she was going next? Did she mention anything on her agenda for the day?"

"No. What's the matter, Chet?"

"She didn't return home last night. It's not like her to be absent without letting me know."

Maxey thought Chet probably needed to be knocked off his self-center every now and then by sisterly lapses such as this. ''If she calls here, I'll tell her to get in touch with you, and you do the same.''

''She absented herself from a CU travel lecture last night, as well. I attended, but I arrived late, waiting for her.''

Maxey wanted to tell him to stop whining, that his sister must have found a more interesting activity and male to do it with. ''Have her call me,'' she said airily, and hung up the phone.

At noon, having written the Gunderloy article without mentioning any Waterfords by name, Maxey drove home to change into a navy dress for the funeral. Timothy and the Ford had already gone, and the garage doors he'd again carelessly left open creaked a lament in the dry breeze.

Planning ahead, Maxey put her 35-mm camera into the Toyota for a run past the Gunderloy after the services. She'd publish a photo of the old house with her article to show she wasn't rousing rabble over some ugly old dump.

Zellerman Funeral Home, one o'clock—that's what Timothy had told her. Parking on the street directly across from the chapel, Maxey wondered if she had misunderstood. The street drowsed, almost empty of cars, and no one stood on the front steps of the steep-roofed brick building.

Shouldering her white purse, she walked to the wide double doors and swung the right one open. The scent of carnations rushed out to meet her. Inside, a rosy-faced, corpulent man, who looked more like a department store Santa than a mortician, motioned Maxey to come in, come in.

"Waterford?" he said, spreading his hand on the nearest polished door in anticipation of her nod. The door swept silently inward and Maxey did the same.

The room, no bigger than Mrs. Waterford's living room, might have been a windowless theater, bathed in rosy light from discreet wall sconces, hushed by the deep wine carpet. About twenty folding chairs faced the center stage—a closed white casket curtained by a huge spill of pink carnations.

Timothy sat, elbows on knees, in the front left corner chair. In the middle of the second row, a knot of elderly ladies murmured and fidgeted. Bailey Marker, natty in a brown suit and bow tie, occupied the far-right-hand seat of the back row.

Wanting to sit with Bailey, Maxey went instead to the front to settle beside Timothy, who did not glance up from his contemplation of the carpet between his scuffed black shoes. He had added a black tweed sports jacket over the rumpled black slacks, along with a blue tie that had an allover pattern of tiny pink pigs, probably the only tie he owned.

Mrs. W. wouldn't have minded.

Maxey had time to wonder which floral arrangement was the one she'd sent, and then someone with squeaky shoes came in from the back and progressed briskly to the front. The minister, by the looks of his band of white collar, smiled out at them before stepping behind a lectern camouflaged by a spray of red roses.

"Friends and loved ones of Elizabeth Hadley Waterford—"

Timothy drew a deep, tremulous breath. Maxey put her hand over his and inwardly flinched at the spongy, hot feel of it.

The service was mercifully short, as was the one at Mountain View Cemetery, where only Timothy, Maxey, and Bailey Marker gathered beside the coffin poised above its grave. Traffic on Highway 119 hummed accompaniment to the minister's clichéd benediction, and gusts of wind tortured the carnations on the casket.

Timothy's eyes gleamed in his pale, damp face, like a zealot's on his way to a witch-hunt.

■

Maxey followed Bailey's blue-green Saturn to Nebraska Street until he turned into his driveway. Parking in front of the Gunderloy, she fiddled with the camera settings longer than would have been necessary if she was a real photographer.

As she exited the car, another car, something bright red, zoomed into the curb in front of Celia's house, and the unmistakable silhouette of Brent the hunk hopped out. He didn't see Maxey wave as he loped up to the front door.

Maxey wandered around the Gunderloy, photographing details, such as the Doric columns holding up the porch roof and the dome-shaped stained-glass window on the second story. To get a shot of the entire front, she had to cross the street to the yard of the burned house, which made her wonder how Calen Taylor's investigation was faring.

Up the street, a second red car arrived at Celia's house and a woman who could have been Monica followed Brent's route to the porch.

Thinking that she would stop in long enough to tell Celia about Elizabeth Waterford's ownership of the Gunderloy, Maxey strolled the half block. The wind continued to roam, shaking trees and scattering dust.

Wiping a strand of hair out of her mouth, Maxey stepped up on Celia's porch and called through the screen door, "Hello, anyone home?"

A droning of male voices went on in the distance. She pushed the doorbell.

"What?" someone shouted.

Before she could answer, Chet arrived at the door. He peered through the screen at her, his face set and sour, as if she was selling something he not only didn't want but didn't approve of.

"I need to see Celia for just a minute," Maxey said, hating the feeling that she was intruding.

"Come in," Chet ordered, rather than invited.

Monica and Brent, both fully, if casually, dressed,

stood in the dim dining room area, faces expectant as they greeted Maxey. Each of them had a canvas bag, their costumes for this afternoon's faux romance, no doubt.

"You know where Celie is?" Brent asked.

"No. Don't you?"

"No. She was going to start a new cover painting today. We agreed on three o'clock. Chet says she hasn't been home since yesterday morning."

Monica walked to the couch and flopped onto it. "It isn't like Celia . . ."

Chet had said the same thing that morning, and Maxey had sloughed it off as Chet's concern for his own welfare rather than for Celia's. Now worry began to knead at her.

"Did she drive somewhere?" Maxey asked.

Chet plowed one hand across the stubble of his hair. "Her automobile and mine are both in the garage."

"Then she must have come home after she stopped in at the *Regard,* because she surely wouldn't have walked all the way from here to Pearl Street. How about a bike?"

"No bicycle. I notified the police immediately this morning, and all they agreed to do was keep an eye out for her . . . as if she were no more than a stray dog."

Maxey felt obligated to stand up for her lover's place of employment. "They can't run around looking for every adult some other adult thinks is missing. We need to find Celia ourselves. How about the foothills area at the end of the street? Does she go hiking up there?''

''Not anymore. She's got arthritis in one knee.'' Chet's thin mouth rolled down at the corners like a baby about to cry.

''Hey, man, we'll find her,'' Brent said, dropping his gym bag and nudging it under the dining room table. ''What was she wearing?''

Chet shrugged. Maxey shut her eyes and pictured Celia marching into the news office to castigate Charles Skye. ''She had a black handbag. A gray-and-white-striped shirt, white slacks, black tennis shoes . . . I think.''

Monica stood up. ''I'll go see if any of that stuff is in her closet.'' She circled around toward the kitchen and disappeared.

''Where else would she have gone on foot?'' Maxey thought out loud.

Brent snapped his fingers. ''The petitions.''

''You're right.'' Maxey turned to Chet. ''How did that work? Was she assigned a certain area to cover—all the neighbors within so many blocks or something?''

''I don't know.''

''Who would know? Who's in charge of the petition drive?''

''I believe Celia is.''

Maxey wondered if Chet had worked up even enough interest to sign the petition. ''Bailey Marker would know,'' she said.

Monica reappeared, her perfect face pinched into a frown. ''This was on the bed.'' She held up the black patchwork bag. ''Her billfold and other stuff are in it.''

Maxey couldn't help throwing Chet an exasperated look. He should have scouted out Celia's room before now.

''I didn't see the clothes you described,'' Monica said. ''I even checked the washer and dryer.''

''Okay, I'll go talk to Bailey. You want to wait for me here?'' Maxey addressed Brent and Monica, having given up on Chet's usefulness.

She found Bailey watering a bed of petunias in front of his little clapboard house. He had removed the suit jacket and the bow tie, and the sleeves of his dress shirt were rolled past the elbows, but his shiny black wing-tip shoes indicated he wasn't serious about yard work.

When Maxey told him about Celia's disappearance, he screwed the water nozzle to off, laid down the hose, and tottered over to sit on the gray concrete porch steps. Maxey wrapped her navy skirt around her knees and sat beside him.

''So how does the petition drive work?'' she asked. ''Is there some way we can find out where Celia's been and where she might be going?''

“Nobody was assigned any particular addresses. You could go anywhere within the city limits. Some petition gatherers station themselves at a busy location, like the public library, and ask every passerby to sign. Celia has been having good luck on Pearl Street Mall, getting all the store owners and their customers.”

“How about right here, in the neighborhood?” Maxey shifted and felt polyester snag on the rough cement.

He smiled a lopsided half smile. “Celia let me get the signatures on Nebraska Street—easy pickings. That way, I could feel like I'd helped.”

“What happens to the petitions after they're signed?”

Bailey rubbed the side of his face with one open palm.

“You mean once a sheet is filled up, what do we do with it? We turn it in to one of the coordinators, a lawyer. His secretary is a notary public. We sign each sheet we turn in, the notary stamps it, and it goes into a file drawer, I guess, till we have enough to file with the city clerk.”

“Great. Then I could find out where Celia's been, and maybe that will tell us where she was going to go next.”

Bailey grunted, his expression doubtful.

Maxey dug into her purse to find her pen and notebook. “Who's the attorney?”

"Ah, Ferry? No, Ferris—Ferric. Ferric, that's it. On Broadway near Mapleton."

"I'll find him. Thanks, Bailey."

"I surely do hope Celia is all right. You hear of so many bad things happening nowadays. Senseless things." He swiveled his neck to survey the charred wreckage of the house next door. The wind stood his thin hair on end until he turned back to her. "Course, there were plenty of bad, senseless things going on in the good old days, too."

Maxey patted his knee and stood up, brushing at her bottom. "Yeah, I've always suspected that 'good old days' was an oxymoron."

Monica opened the door before Maxey could rap on it. "Chet's fixing coffee," she said, leading off through the dining area to the kitchen.

In reality, Brent was making the coffee while Chet sat on a stool at the breakfast bar, staring into space.

"Has Mr. Marker seen Celia lately?" Brent asked, scooping coffee granules.

"No. He gave me the name of the man who would know where she's been petitioning. Let's hope there's some kind of pattern in that so we can guess where she'd have petitioned next."

"When you get the information, call me," Monica said, digging into her jeans pocket to produce a business card to hand to Maxey.

"Let me give you my number, too," Brent said, taking the card from Maxey's fingers and flipping it over to scribble on the back with a ballpoint pen from his shirt pocket.

"Chet?" Maxey said, handing him the card and motioning for Brent to share the pen.

Chet blinked and focused on her face. "What?"

"Give me your work number."

Instead of taking the proffered card and pen, he slowly stood, one hand flat on the countertop as if to keep from falling. "I didn't kill her," he said in a voice as hollow as an empty room.

■

Maxey thought of Chet's spooky eyes and spookier words as she walked up one flight of curved oak stairs to the offices of Aaron Ferric. The shocked little silence that followed Chet's declaration had seemed to bring him back to his senses. Laughing an insincere laugh, he said that he'd wanted to kill her often enough when they were kids, so now that she had disappeared, he felt compelled to deny responsibility.

Brent and Monica had dredged up smiles. But Maxey was too busy wondering if Chet had failed to find Celia's purse because he hadn't looked into Celia's room because he knew damn well what had happened to her.

At the top of the steps, a gleaming hardwood floor led past old-fashioned doors with frosted-glass windows. From behind one of them came an electric typewriter's authoritative chatter. Otherwise, the hall lay secretive and still. Maxey felt constrained to tiptoe along the creaking gauntlet as she read the brass plates screwed to the walls beside the doors.

Aaron T. Ferric, Attorney at Law, should be behind door number four. Wondering if she was supposed to knock, Maxey rotated the knob and walked in.

The receptionist's desk, a mostly empty walnut top with its inevitable computer terminal centerpiece, was womaned by a slender young lady wearing an electric blue dress and an aura of department store perfume.

"Hello. May I help you?" she said, resting her fingers on the keyboard and smiling up at Maxey.

"This is my business card. Please ask Mr. Ferric if he could see me for a moment about a mutual friend who seems to be missing."

The receptionist snapped the edge of the card back and forth with her long red thumbnail. "He's with a client right now. Would you like to wait?"

"I would."

Maxey sank into one of four mauve-upholstered armchairs ranged at right angles to the desk. She took a cursory inventory of the magazines splayed on the glass-topped table by her elbow—*ABA Journal, The Docket, Lawyer's Monthly*—not a *People* or a *National Enquirer* in sight. Maxey opened her purse and dug through the jumbled contents, searching for her notebook.

"Maybe I could help you."

The young man standing in front of her, hands in the pockets of his tan slacks, smiled hopefully. His light yellow shirt was open and tieless. His loafers needed polish and his ankles needed socks.

"You're not Mr. Ferric," Maxey felt confident in guessing.

"I'm his secretary, Kerry Atwood."

"Maxey Burnell. Are you a notary? The one who officiates over the Gunderloy petitions?"

"Right. I am. I do."

"Good. Maybe I won't have to bother Mr. Ferric. I'm here because Celia Vogle—you know Celia?"

He nodded.

"She's disappeared, possibly while gathering petitions."

Kerry lunged into the chair beside her and crossed one knee over the other, looking very relaxed and ready to listen. His left earlobe bore the blemish of a piercing he'd since abandoned.

Maxey told him about Celia and about the possibility of determining where she was when she disappeared by studying the petitions she'd been gathering. During Maxey's recitation, the fragrant receptionist uttered a low exclamation and came around her desk to join them.

''That nice Ms. Vogle?'' she said, hugging herself. ''Oh, how awful.''

''We can sort out her petitions from everyone else's. Put them in order by date. Is that what you need?'' Kerry asked.

''That's exactly it. Could I have photocopies of them?''

Ferric's employees frowned at each other, not sure.

''If I can just make some notes,'' Maxey said, ''that's good enough. And could I borrow a phone book? For the city map in back?''

Half an hour later, seated at a long table in a back room, with Celia's petitions spread out in a rough semicircle, Maxey dropped her pen and slumped in the hard plastic chair, amazed.

''How're you doing?''

She turned, expecting to see Kerry. Instead, a gentleman with graying black hair, a ski-slope sharp nose, and a paunch as impressive as an eighth-month pregnancy lounged in the doorway.

''Mr. Ferric?''

''Ms. Burnell. Kerry told me what you're doing. That's bad news about Celia. Have the police been called in on it?''

''Yes, but you know they don't get immediately involved unless there's an obvious indication of foul play. I appreciate the help I've been given here. And look at this. I didn't expect it to be so easy . . . so obvious.'' She flipped her notebook open to the page she'd filled with addresses. ''Celia gathered signatures on Pearl Street May tenth, twelfth, fifteenth, sixteenth—every day or every other day up through the thirtieth, the last day you have a sheet of petitions from her.''

Maxey hadn't meant ''look at this'' literally. Since her notes were so messy, she could scarcely read them herself. However, Ferric had obediently crossed to stand beside her, his knuckles braced on the tabletop, his breathing rough and redolent of stale tobacco.

''Most days, she was also stopping door-to-door on residential streets,'' Maxey said, tapping the phone book, which lay open to the shiny pastel map of Boulder's northwest corner. ''All the addresses are in this part of town, near where Celia lives. The numbered streets, Fourth, Fifth, and so on, don't tell us anything, because she was using them as cross streets, and they show up throughout her petitions. But if you list the east-west streets, starting with May eleventh, she petitioned on Balsam, Cedar, Dellwood, Evergreen, Forest, Grape—'' Maxey's forefinger ticked up the map from south to north in perfect chronological order.

''Huh,'' Ferric grunted. ''Hawthorne Street on Saturday, which is the last petition page she turned in. And the next street would be—huh! Nebraska.''

''Bailey Marker already collected the signatures on Nebraska Street.'' Maxey drew her fingernail under the next street north of that. ''Applewood. Want to place any bets?''

11

■ ■ ■

Applewood, the first street north of Nebraska, offered the same eclectic mixture of large and small, old and older homes with neat or neglected lawns. Monica, Brent, and Maxey huddled at the Ninth Street intersection as the day began to fade into dusk. Chet had been assigned telephone duty, waiting at home for any calls from or about his sister.

"Maybe we should have phoned Gary. To help us canvass," Maxey said.

"Gary?" As if it was still broad daylight, Monica shaded her eyes to look up the street.

"Isn't that his name? The other model Celia uses."

"He's out of town," Brent said. "I think. Well, hell, all right, he and Celia had a falling-out."

"A falling-out? What about?"

Brent scuffed his sneaker toe in the sand on the sidewalk. "He wanted more money to pose for her, or something. Look, how about if I take Ninth up to the next corner, both sides?''

''How about if I go east on Applewood to Broadway and back?'' Monica slapped at her arm, bare below the white T-shirt sleeve. ''Rats. I should have brought mosquito repellent.''

''Okay. And I'll go west on Applewood. Meet back here when we can?'' Maxey suggested, and the other two nodded before setting off in the agreed directions.

Maxey walked west, up the gradual incline toward the foothills dead end. Turning into the first driveway on the south side, she scooped up the rolled newspaper lying there and carried it to the front door.

A middle-aged woman wearing a business suit answered Maxey's ring and accepted her newspaper delivery without smiling, the image of a wary homeowner who had better things to do than listen to a sales pitch on her porch.

''My friend Celia Vogle lives on the street behind you,'' Maxey began. ''And she's disappeared. Could you tell me if she came here to ask for your signature on a petition yesterday afternoon or evening?''

The woman's face relaxed. She touched the back of her hair, swept up in a knot that was coming unraveled. ''No. No one came here yesterday at all. Sorry, I can't help you.''

''I'm sorry, too. Thanks anyway.''

''What does she look like?''

"Blond. About my size. About forty years old. She was probably wearing white slacks and shirt."

The woman shook her head one time, making her hair slip and slide. "Didn't see her. Of course, I might not have been home from work yet, if it was about this time of evening."

"What about your husband? Children? Anyone else who might have been home when she knocked?"

"Not yesterday."

It was the same at the next house and the next two after that. Everyone seemed to have a job outside the home, and no one had seen Celia.

At the fifth house, a self-important toddler in a clattering Big Wheel zoomed across Maxey's path. He or she looked back across a bare golden-brown shoulder blade to check the stranger's reaction. Maxey smiled, and, thus encouraged, the child peddled furiously up the driveway to have another pass at her.

"Josh," a female voice shouted from the porch.

Josh careened past Maxey and cranked a hard right turn that mired him against the edge of the front lawn.

"Hello." Maxey took advantage of the sudden silence to call to the woman. "May I ask you a question?"

The woman, who had a thicket of white-blond hair and a Rubenesque body in halter and shorts, stood at the top of the porch steps, studying Maxey as she hiked the last few feet of driveway.

"Excuse me for bothering you, but one of your neighbors has disappeared, and I'm wondering if you might have seen her yesterday."

"Yeah? Who?"

"Celia Vogle."

"Oh, she's not my neighbor. She lives way over on the next street." The woman unself-consciously lifted an arm and scratched at her armpit.

"Celia might have been on Applewood yesterday collecting petitions for the Gunderloy house."

"The what? Oh, you mean that big old place at the end of the street." She gestured vaguely west.

"Yes. You must be able to see the Gunderloy's backyard from your backyard."

"I guess," the woman said, as if she'd never actually noticed.

Josh, struggling to back out of the grass and realign his vehicle on the driveway, raised a shrill demand that Mom come and help.

Ignoring him, Mom lifted one bare foot and examined the sole. "Nope, I haven't seen her. She's probably off in Las Vegas with a married man."

"Was Celia having a relationship like that?" Maxey asked, startled.

"Darned if I know." The woman frowned out at Josh, who had managed to free the Big Wheel and now dragged it between his knees along the driveway.

Maxey thanked her and, giving Josh a wide berth, trudged toward the street and turned west.

"You going next door?" Josh's mother called.

"I'm trying every house on the block." Maxey stopped walking to answer.

"They aren't home. Come back here and let me tell you—I can save you a bunch of time."

Maxey didn't appreciate being ordered around in the same tone of voice Mom used on Josh. Nevertheless, she retraced her steps. Josh climbed off the Big Wheel and solemnly watched her arrival.

"These people here," his mother said, waving at the next house, "they're out of town. The next house up, they're gone, too. The last house, up on the hill, it's for sale. Empty. Over there"—she pointed—"they work till one o'clock week mornings." She continued to indicate houses and reveal their late-afternoon vulnerabilities to complete stranger Maxey, who listened, both aghast at and grateful for the confidence.

Two houses across the street would be occupied now and probably were occupied yesterday at this or a later hour.

"I appreciate your helping me," Maxey said. "You might not want to tell just anybody about your neighbors' comings and goings. I'm not a burglar, but—"

''Well, of course you aren't. Josh, you get that finger out of your nose before I chop it off.''

Maxey withdrew, heading for the two indicated houses.

Five minutes later, having collected two more negative answers to her question about Celia, she trudged east to rendezvous with Brent and Monica. Arriving first, thanks to the shortcut Josh's mom had provided, Maxey stood under a stuttering streetlamp and battled mosquitoes. She felt moderately optimistic that Brent or Monica would have found Celia's trail. But when they arrived within seconds of one another, Brent whistling something low and sad and Monica limping from a blister on her heel, neither of them had talked to anyone who remembered Celia.

■

''How's your cold?''

''What cold?''

''Last night on the phone, you thought you were catching a cold.''

''Oh, yeah. I guess it was just an allergy,'' Sam said.

Maxey waited a beat to give him time to invite himself over.

''So why'd you call?'' he said.

Depression settled over her like smog. She considered simply hanging up. Giving herself a mental shake, she asked, ''Had you heard about my preservationist friend Celia Vogle being missing?''

''No. Tell me about it.''

So she did, right up to the part where, half an hour ago, she'd left Chet sitting on his couch with a full whiskey bottle between his knees.

''He didn't seem at all surprised we'd found no sign of Celia. He seems to have made up his mind that she's dead. He keeps trying to make lame jokes about how he didn't do it.''

''He doth protest too much, huh?''

''Maybe. Got any ideas what we should do next?''

''I'll look into it tomorrow, see if the guys have been investigating on it at all.''

''I can't believe I was wrong about the petitions. She never went more than a day or two without collecting some signatures, and her clipboard's missing. She must have been walking around knocking on doors Monday afternoon or evening, and the logical place is Applewood Street.''

''You said she started on the south and worked north to Nebraska.''

''Right.''

''Maybe Nebraska was her line of demarcation or something. Maybe when she reached it, she planned to begin at some northern point and work her way south to Nebraska again.''

Maxey thought about it. ''Wouldn't she have taken the car, then?''

"I don't know. She's your friend. How far would she have been willing to walk?"

"I don't know, either." Maxey sighed, rubbing at the pucker of frown line between her eyebrows. "I'll check out your theory tomorrow. Except—how do I know which street is the northernmost starting line?"

"Find out which street was her southernmost starting line and count the number of streets up to Nebraska. Then count the same number from Nebraska northward." He yawned hugely.

"Guess I'd better let you go," she said.

The six words echoed in her head the rest of the evening, like a maudlin country song.

■

Wednesday morning, Maxey punched her office key into the door lock an hour earlier than usual. All the work she should have done Tuesday afternoon would be lying in wait on her desk. Thursday's camera-ready newspaper needed to be at the printer's by three o'clock today. Her renewed search for Celia would have to be on hold till late afternoon.

Maxey managed to harvest two hours of fruitful labor before Reece arrived. As independent and disorganized as he appeared to be, Reece always rose to the occasion of a deadline. He knew what to do, and, like most lazy men, he knew how to do it with the least amount of wasted effort. Maxey never felt closer to her ex-husband than on Wednesdays while the two of them slaved over a hot *Regard.*

■

"O'Meara."

"Here-a."

"Patterson."

"Right here."

Tilt cleaned under one fingernail with the smaller blade of his pocketknife. Two number-two pencils lay in readiness for today's promised essay test. Most of Vogle's tests were a snap. The trick to getting *A*'s was to parrot the same pretentious words the professor used himself: *epiphany, paradigm, syntonic, dystopia.* Make your answer abstruse enough, the old guy probably creamed his pants.

"Tilton."

"Here."

"Waterford. Waterford? No?"

The professor didn't look so hot today. Or rather, he looked too hot. His face shone with perspiration, and his eyes wandered, unfocused and wet. Maybe Vogle was coming down with the flu. Maybe he'd tipped the old stein one too many times last night.

Now he leaned over his lectern and shook a sheaf of papers at the nearest female student. She took her time about getting to her feet to accept the exams and pass them out.

Tilt touched the knife blade to the edge of the

desktop in front of his belt buckle and pressed until the wood gave way. He wished that it was night and he was prowling along some stranger's sidewalk, can of gasoline in hand, about to fill the dark with light and sirens and drama.

The girl with the exams handed him one. Closing and pocketing the knife, he bent to read the first question. "Discuss the difference between sexist stereotypes and sexual archetypes in modern sword-and-sorcery novelization."

Tilt grunted and began to write. "Stereotype paradigms oversimplify the dystopia involved in sword-and-sorcery epiphanies."

The continuous shuffle of papers and feet sounded like the rustle of newborn fire.

■

By skipping lunch, Maxey and Reece had the paper whipped into shape by 2:40. She volunteered to run it to the printers and bring back sandwiches from the deli.

At 3:20, Maxey returned, white sacks in hand. "Morrie saved us the last two sandwich specials of the day—barbecued liver on sourdough."

Reece took his sack between thumb and forefinger, holding it well away from him. "What are they really?"

"Fish pastrami on pumpernickel. Eat up."

"You're in a good mood." He inspected the interior of the sandwich and apparently recognized it as edible. Around a big mouthful, he mumbled, ''Missed you yesterday.''

''I didn't expect to be gone so long. What with one thing or another, I didn't get the photo developed to go with my Gunderloy story.'' She popped the lid off her iced tea and dumped in some sweetener. ''Did I tell you that Mrs. Waterford was the owner of the Gunderloy house? You know, the place that Celia and her friends are trying to save.''

Reece shook his head. His cheek swelled as he tucked a bite of sandwich in it and took a swallow of coffee.

''Yeah, and, Reece, there's a good chance that Mrs. Waterford was deliberately run over. Murdered.''

Unable to speak, he swayed his head and rolled his eyes.

''I think Timothy ought to lead the fight to preserve the Gunderloy. Make it sort of a memorial to his grandmother.''

''Timoffy,'' Reece said, and gestured with his sandwich.

''Yeah, it would give him something to do besides mourn. And I'll tell you something else, Reece. If it was murder, I'm not going to let the murderer get away with it.''

The rest room's toilet flushed. Maxey froze, paper cup of tea halfway to her mouth.

"Hear, hear!" Timothy shouted, coming from the back. "You'll have all the bad guys shaking in their size tens."

Maxey glared at Reece, who shrugged. "I tried to tell you," he said, cramming the last of his sandwich into his mouth.

"Sorry, Timothy. I didn't know you were here. But I mean it. I'm not going to forget your grandmother. And I mean it about the Gunderloy, too. If you've inherited it, you could do wonderful things, beginning with telling Skye and Skye to jump in a cold lake."

"Boy, she knows how to raise rabble," Timothy said to Reece.

"She does," he agreed, wiping his hands down his jeans legs. "She's got the bite of a Komodo dragon—gets a problem in her jaws and never lets go. A year ago, she captured a wanted man single-handed. Went to his motel room to make a citizen's arrest, and when he wouldn't come peaceably, she beat him senseless with her brassiere."

Timothy laughed, but his eyes remained wary. "You're putting me on."

"No, it's true." Reece warded off Maxey's attempts to shush him. "She put some plumbing in her bra and—ouch. See how feisty and determined she is?"

Timothy stared at her, adding to Maxey's embarrassment. "He'd murdered his wife, sort of a friend of mine,'' she tried to explain. ''I found out, so he thought he had to kill me, too. I just got lucky. Unlucky, and then lucky.''

Reece leaned toward Timothy to stage-whisper behind his hand. ''She packs a thirty-four-caliber cup.''

''You're dangerously close to sexual harassment, Macy.'' Maxey stomped away to deposit the dregs of lunch in a trash can.

Behind her, Reece continued his confidence. ''Believe me, Waterford, she won't rest till she gets all the answers to everything.''

''So, Maxey,'' Timothy called, ''how about taking my speculative fiction makeup exam?''

Wiping her hands and her mouth, Maxey rejoined the men, determined to change the subject. ''Who's your instructor? Chet Vogle?''

''Yeah. You know him?''

''Slightly. What's he like?''

Timothy spent several seconds considering his cast. It was beginning to fray around the edges, Maxey noticed, and no one had autographed it.

''What's Vogle like?'' Timothy mused. ''Moody. Pompous. No sense of humor whatsoever. If you know him slightly, that's as close as you want to get.''

''Think he could commit a murder?'' Maxey said, and immediately wished she hadn't.

Reece stiffened his spine and frowned at her.

''You mean Grandmother?'' Timothy said incredulously.

''No, just a hypothetical murder. Forget I asked. It was a dumb thing to—''

''Who's the hypothetical victim?'' Timothy persisted.

''Well, um, his sister is missing.''

''His sister.'' Timothy seemed intrigued by this exercise in suppositions. ''What does she look like?''

Maxey rattled off Celia's vital statistics without having to think, she'd done it so often lately. ''Recognize her?''

''Uh-uh, nope. But now that I know, if I see her, I'll tell her you want her.''

He'd been leaning against Reece's desk; now he circled it to drop into the nearest chair. Maxey thought he looked thinner than he had when they met. His pale, sad face sagged like a bloodhound's.

''When was the last time you ate?'' she asked, ready to be scandalized by the answer.

''I'm okay, Maxey. Stop fussing.''

''He came in to work,'' Reece said. ''Right after we put the paper to bed. Great timing, Waterford.''

''There's a box of cookies in the cupboard over the coffeemaker,'' Maxey said.

Reece twisted around to wink at Timothy. ''What did I tell you? You'd better have a cookie so the Komodo dragon will leave you alone.''

■

Komodo dragon Burnell stood at the intersection of Ninth and Applewood and waited for some kind of sign. The fading light of dusk softened the neighborhood like a sepia photograph. Someone's beef barbecue scented the air with its mouthwatering perfume. Someone else's wind chimes chinged a torturous two notes. A dark automobile mumbled by, turning into a driveway on Ninth.

In a test of Sam's theory that Celia might have started petitioning at the northern limits of her chosen territory, Monica and Brent had elected to knock on doors on Poplar Avenue tonight.

''I'll meet you somewhere up there later,'' Maxey had said. ''First I want to take another look at Applewood.''

''You think someone will be home tonight who wasn't home last night?'' Monica asked.

''I skipped about six places at the end of the street because this one woman told me the houses aren't occupied. That was dumb. What if Celia went to a vacant house and fell down the porch steps or something?''

''Oh, yeah, you'd better check it out.''

So now Maxey walked west toward the dead end of Applewood and its foothills barricade. A man she'd spoken to the night before nodded as he strode from garage to house. A cat that she'd petted minced daintily into her path to claim another stroke.

Maxey quickened her pace past Josh's house, where open windows leaked the unmistakable sounds of loony tunes and merry melodies. The blue-and-white clapboard house next door looked as deserted as Josh's mom had proclaimed it would be. When Maxey rang the doorbell, nothing inside stirred or shifted.

She cut across the grass to reach the neighboring driveway, then across that to the stepping-stones that pointed toward the front stoop. Except for a robin scolding in a lilac bush, this place seemed deserted, too. When she pushed the bell, Maxey couldn't hear it ring inside the house, so she knocked, as well. When nothing happened, she called, "Celia?" and, feeling foolish, retreated to the street again.

The sidewalk rose sharply, and then it and the street deteriorated into gravel that slithered and slipped under Maxey's shoes, slowing her upward march. Apparently, Applewood ended in wild, steep private property. An aluminum country mailbox on a splintered wooden post marked where the street fizzled out and the driveway began. Unkempt trees and bushes bristled from the weedy embankment, hiding the house.

About to lean into the climb, Maxey stopped instead and screwed her sneaker toes into the shifting surface while she fought an attack of premonition. Near the mailbox, a red-white-and-blue sign had been pounded into the rocky hillside. HERE'S ANOTHER FINE DEVELOPMENT, it said. SKYE AND SKYE.

12

■ ■ ■

Maxey's breathing came in lung-pinching gasps by the time she reached the top of the drive and stopped to survey the house. It should have been a big veranda-wrapped mansion to match the wide, secretive yard. Instead, a modest, to the point of self-effacing, one-story perched there, its mean little front porch like an afterthought tacked to one side. One multipaned window faced front beside the aluminum storm door. Ivy crept across the two steps to the porch, slowly establishing squatters' rights.

She imagined she could smell decay lapping against the foundation.

"Celia?" Maxey strained her ears for any answering call, cough, or groan. Far in the distance, a baritone dog barked and barked.

Sighing, Maxey circled around to the side, where a line of windows trooped front to back with military precision. Hanging by her fingertips from the stone sills and hopping awkwardly in place, she was able to see inside, one window after another: an empty front room, an empty middle room. An almost-empty bedroom with only the bed frame to identify it, a kitchen gray with dust.

The windows ran out, and an unkempt spruce tree, swaying and whispering in the steady breeze, barred Maxey's forward progress. Circling the tree, she found herself on the crest of the backyard, staring down at a black iron fence that separated this property from its Nebraska Street neighbor. The roof of that neighbor rose in interesting peaks, the most interesting being one resembling a witch's hat. Maxey recognized the little back porch where she'd peered inside at a kitchen full of ghosts.

No wonder Skye and Skye wanted the Gunderloy. Since they already owned the real estate behind it, acquiring the Gunderloy could at least double the size of their condominium plans.

She didn't have time to ponder all of the ramifications. The light was failing fast, and she hadn't thought to bring along a flashlight. Turning around, she considered the rear of the Applewood house. It towered over her, seemingly bigger because of the way the ground fell away here. The back porch, more generous than the front one, struggled to rise above the bushes and vines that surrounded it.

While Maxey puzzled over a black stain on one of the columns that held up the roof, the southwestern breeze that had been steadily teasing her hair suddenly stopped. In the still, oppressive void, a subtle odor settled over the scene—an acrid, burnt-meat smell—that sent apprehension swooping through Maxey's stomach.

She swallowed hard, struggling against the desire to retreat before she could see something she would never be able to forget. She could go for help. Let someone else investigate the looming, shadowed porch. But what if it was only some small varmint that had died here? How could she call the police before she knew that this situation warranted their time and trouble?

She fumbled the tail of her shirt out of her jeans and pressed it over her mouth and nose.

A wooden lattice skirted the crawl space under the porch. It would have been invisible behind the greenery, except the greenery had turned to brown below the blackened porch support. The blasted plants revealed a hole in the lattice, large enough for Maxey to crawl through if she was that hungry for information. It took all of her willpower to squat and look through the hole.

The dark heap might have been an old blanket or a pile of laundry or even a hibernating bear. But none of those would have explained the clipboard lying beside it, scraps of scorched petition paper still attached.

Maxey exhaled a long, shaky breath. "Oh, Celia." Gritting her teeth, she squirmed into the gap in the lattice and stretched to touch the nearest body part, a knee, apparently, drawn up in fetal position. The cloth enshrouding it was cool and damp, but not as cool as Maxey had expected.

"Celia?"

Her hope being stronger than her horror, she lay down and used her elbows to drag her in beside Celia. It was impossible to see Celia's face. Her head was a black shadow that smelled of scorched hair and gasoline.

With a reluctant hand, Maxey touched Celia's slumped shoulder, then traced its slope down to find her chilly neck. Pressing fingers lightly against it, Maxey held her breath. Was the feathery beat that she felt her own heart or Celia's?

She shifted, about to put her other hand on her own neck to check her heart's rhythm, and Celia sighed—a soft, final sound, like the last drops of water slipping down a drain.

"Oh! Oh God. I'll be back, Celia. Hang on. It's going to be okay." Maxey's voice bumped up and down with her frantic, backward crawling.

Emerging into the anemic sunlight, she didn't hesitate. Instead of retracing her route to Applewood Street, Maxey rushed headlong down the hill to climb the iron fence—fortunately, it wasn't high or spiked. Running through the Gunderloy yard, she was thankful to see a light glowing in Bailey

Marker's front window. Bailey would be better than Chet in this—or probably any—emergency.

She rushed his porch, ricocheted off the front door frame, and shouted through the screen. "Bailey, it's Maxey. I need you to phone nine-one-one. I've found Celia. Give me some blankets—she's alive."

Bailey came at a fast shuffle to unhook the door. "Take them off that bed," he said, pointing at the hallway. He raised his voice as Maxey rushed to the four-poster bed and dug beneath the faded quilt for an armload of blue wool blankets. "Where is she?"

She told him, already halfway out the front door, Bailey already dialing.

■

"Is there one chance in the world that it could be coincidence? The two women with the most interest in the Gunderloy, both involved in violence within days of each other? Is it feasibly, conceivably possible that there's no connection between the attacks?"

Bailey shrugged, his watery eyes gazing into space. He'd settled into a worn-looking Boston rocker at one end of the antique gateleg that served as his kitchen table. The rest of the room matched the chair—cracked oilcloth on the table, walnut cupboards parched for furniture polish, linoleum with a no-longer-legible pattern. Through the uncurtained window above the sink came the sharp essence of skunk.

"You can't tell me that there's no connection," Maxey said. "The Gunderloy may not be the cause, but it's got to be the common denominator."

Bailey patted at his breast pocket and brought out a box of thin cigars, which he gallantly offered for Maxey's refusal before selecting and lighting his own. The sweet, hot chocolaty scent freshened the room.

"I ought to go back to Applewood and gather information for the *Regard*," she said without moving.

A minute clicked over on the digital clock above the refrigerator.

Suddenly, Maxey envisioned Monica and Brent, knocking on doors in the north part of town. "I have to go, Bailey."

He breathed out a smoky sigh. The rocker began to squeak. Maxey jumped up and rinsed her coffee cup before she could change her mind about returning to the real world.

"If you hear anything from the hospital, give me a call," Bailey said.

"You, too. Don't get up. I can find the front door."

"Keep a weather eye open, Maxey."

Maxey's vision blurred instead as she passed through the living room on her way out. Bailey's upholstered furniture wore antimacassar crowns.

There were two police cars in front of Chet's house, and every window blazed with light.

■

Brent and Monica sat side by side in an orange plastic booth at Digby's Den. Maxey slid in opposite, and they both stared at her, anxious for the latest progress report from the hospital.

"No change. It's a coma, but they can't say how long it might last."

"So what, exactly, happened to her?" Monica asked, pushing her beer mug around in circles.

"Someone hit her on the back of the head. Then her attacker apparently tried to set her on fire."

Brent moaned and wiped one hand down his face. Monica swung the glass mug up and took a hefty drink. When she set it down again, her wet eyes glittered.

"Did Celia have a significant other?" Maxey asked, mindful of how often a passionate love skidded into an even more passionate hate.

Monica frowned. Brent started to speak, compressed his mouth, and picked up his beer.

"Come on, Brent, give," Maxey said.

"He wasn't very significant, but she did have a thing for Gary for a while."

"Gary?" Maxey tried to picture brisk, practical Celia and pretty boy Gary sharing an embrace like the ones that Celia painted.

"It wasn't, you know, an affair to remember," Monica said. Her mascara had smeared a black tear at the outer corner of each eye. ''Celia dated a lot of guys, but none of them got serious, and neither did she. She told me once that she liked the idea of mellowing into a spinster in a house that she had decorated herself—surrounded by books and records, going where she wanted, doing what she wanted. The typical merry widow without the messy preliminaries.''

Maxey swallowed Coors past the lump in her throat.

''That Skye character is on the top of my suspect list,'' Brent said, tracing the rim of his mug with a forefinger, the other arm draped on the back of the seat behind Monica. ''See, the old lady owner of the Gunderloy must have decided not to sell to him, and he figured her grandson would be easier to convince. Skye probably didn't run over her himself. Rich guys hire that kind of job out.''

Monica folded her arms on the table, hunching her shoulders up around her ears. ''So then what? Maybe Celia found out about it? Or maybe she just accused Skye of something that came too close to the truth. So he tried to kill her too.''

''There's no point in speculating yet,'' Maxey said. ''Not till we get the police report and talk to Celia. There may be a whole slew of suspects we know nothing about right now.''

''Maybe Chet did it,'' Brent said, ignoring

Maxey's advice. ''To take over his sister's share of the house and money.''

''What's that got to do with Mrs. Waterford?'' Monica asked.

''Oh. Yeah. Well, then maybe her getting run down really *was* an accident.''

''We're wasting our time,'' Maxey complained. ''I'm going home.'' She slapped a five-dollar bill in the center of the table and slid out of the booth, shrugging the strap of her shoulder bag into place.

''Let us know what you find out from the police tomorrow,'' Monica called after her.

Maxey waved, her answering voice no match for the boisterous camaraderie of a crowd of young men around the dartboard beside the bar.

■

After two hours of trying to sleep, three hours of sleep, and two hours of trying to wake up, Maxey rolled out of the mussed bed to face Thursday.

She wanted to call Sam and discuss Celia, but he wasn't at the station, and he didn't answer at home. Next she tried Reece, who should be up and dressed and on his way out the door to the office but who would, she knew, be none of the above.

''Hmph?'' he answered from someplace deep and dark.

''I have to do something this morning. Could you please open the office?''

"What? Again? Maxey, this is getting to be a bad habit."

"Two times in three hundred and sixty-five days is not a habit."

"So what do you have to do? Shave your legs? Change Moe's litter box?"

"I've got a story to research. Reece, someone tried to murder Celia Vogle."

"My gosh."

"She was found at a deserted house up behind the Gunderloy mansion. Well, actually *I* found her."

Reece muttered words of disbelief and sympathy. "You know, Maxey, no offense, but . . . you sure seem to attract trouble. I'm wondering if I shouldn't sell you my share of the paper and get out from under your bad karma."

"You're always threatening to sell me your share, and karma or no karma, the answer is go fish."

"Spoken like a true CEO."

"It's late, Reece. Open the *Regard*, huh? I'll be in after I check out the crime scene."

"Watch yourself. If you hear any sinister background music, run like hell."

■

Feeling a strong sense of déjà vu, Maxey parked the Toyota at the end of Applewood Street, behind a Boulder Fire Department car. Circumventing the yellow plastic tape stretched across the driveway, she hiked up the grade past the ANOTHER FINE DEVELOPMENT sign. The morning, already too warm, smelled like moldy grass clippings.

She came into view of the ugly little front porch, which seemed to beckon like a mousetrap for her investigation. As she had the day before, Maxey hurried by it. Along the side of the house, past the chain of blank windows, around the blowsy evergreen, she walked with reluctant purposefulness.

A man knelt beside the blackened hole in the porch lattice. Hearing Maxey, he settled back on his heels and looked around to see who had come.

"Hi, Calen. Remember me? Maxey Burnell."

He nodded and blotted his face against his sleeve. With his gray shirt and pants and his salt-and-pepper hair, he matched his smoky surroundings. "Out for a morning jog?"

"Out looking for a policeman, but you'll do. Is it okay if I watch and ask some questions?"

"Have a seat." He motioned to the bottom porch step. It occurred to Maxey that she'd been sitting on more than her share of porch steps lately. This one was tan stone, worn as smooth as a cabochon by countless shoe soles.

"You're investigating the fire part of this attempted murder?" Maxey asked. "What do you know so far?"

"It's messy. Very much the work of an amateur. You sure you want to hear?"

She wasn't, but she nodded.

''Ms. Vogle was stuffed under the porch, a bath towel was saturated in gasoline and wrapped around her head, and then it was set on fire.''

Maxey tilted her neck back and stared into the cottonwood branches overhanging the house. The leaves shivered and swayed in a breeze that didn't touch her face. For a few weak moments, she considered selling her share of the *Regard* to Reece and taking her karma to Australia to begin anew.

''Calen, do you think whoever did this had anything to do with the fire over on Nebraska Street?''

''Except for the location and the use of gasoline, there's not much similarity. The Nebraska Street arsonist broke in and doused the downstairs. Here, the house wasn't entered, and there was so little gasoline used, the fire went out almost immediately. The charring you see here on the porch support and floor—that's the extent of it.''

She wrapped her arms around her legs and smiled at him. ''Any fingerprints?''

''The police are checking on that this time. I still don't have a name to go with the one on the pickle jar, and no suspect. My job's a lot like reading a terrific thriller and finding that the last chapter is missing.''

''How would you plot out this thriller?'' Maxey nodded at the gaping flaw in the lattice. ''Why did this character do that to Celia?''

Calen peeled off his rubber gloves and flexed his fingers before answering. "Sociopath. He's got to be."

■

Timothy began his first hours of real work for the *Regard* by volunteering to solicit advertising at Crossroads Mall, endearing himself to Maxey, and especially to Reece, whose turn it was to do it. Timothy returned after three hours, triumphantly bearing eleven new sales contracts and one JC Penney sweatshirt on sale for half price.

Periodically through the day, Maxey phoned Boulder Community to ask about Celia. The responses might as well have been recordings, always the same—no change. Celia was alive and stable, but she continued comatose.

"How badly is she burned?" Maxey asked the first time she called for a progress report.

"Ms. Vogle has second and third degree burns over ten percent of her body."

Maxey squeezed her eyes shut. Maybe it was a blessing that Celia hadn't wakened to reality yet.

At the end of the working day, after Reece and Timothy went home, Maxey settled deeper into her chair and dialed the police. Out of habit, she asked for Sam.

"Russell," he answered, sounding in a hurry.

Maxey deliberately leaned back in her chair and

planted both feet on top of her desk. The pose was uncomfortable, but it made a statement.

''Hi. Do you know anything about the Vogle case?''

''What do you want to know, Max?''

''For starters, what was the weapon?''

''Unknown. Nothing at the crime scene matched the description of the wound. It was something big and heavy, like a baseball bat. Maybe a tree branch. Got her low at the base of the skull.''

''Had she been sexually assaulted?''

''No.''

One small favor to be thankful for.

''Was she struck down where I found her?''

''Indications are she was dragged up the hill from the Gunderloy backyard.''

''Whoa. Then my theory about her being on Aplewood to collect petitions was all wrong.''

''Yeah, but whatever works. You found her for us.''

''Any clues? Fingerprints? How about on her clipboard, if her attacker carried it up the hill, too?''

''It was wiped clean. The perp may be crazy, but he's not out of his mind.'' Sam sighed. ''If there was any other clue, we missed it. Don't print that.''

''When did all this happen?''

Paper rustled. ''Monday night, it looks like.''

Monday—the day Celia had lambasted Charles Skye in the *Regard* office, the day Maxey first considered that Mrs. Waterford's death might be murder. Maxey lifted her feet off the desk and squirmed straight in her chair, feeling better in an odd sort of way. What the hell if Sam was slowly backing out of her life? Where was the tragedy in a love affair gone bad when any given breath might be one's last?

"Does Chet have an alibi for Monday night?"

"At a lecture. He could have done it before or after, I've no doubt. Why? You know something we don't?"

"No, it's just that . . . well, when we first started searching for her, he said, 'I didn't kill her.' Seemed like kind of a funny thing to say."

"Is that how he said it? You put emphasis on *I* and on *her.*"

"Well, come to think of it, that's how he did say it. Oh my gosh. That sounds like he did kill someone, but not Celia."

"Sounds pretty flimsy to me."

"Yeah, I guess. But I wonder where he was when Mrs. Waterford was hit."

"How about leaving the snooping to the police, huh? You know, Max, we should maybe go over your statement, see if there's anything you can add while things are fresh in your mind. You want to come in and do that tomorrow?"

"No. I'll let you know if I think of anything," she said, depression again weighing on her like armor. "I might be catching a cold myself."

Much later, she arrived home with two sacks of groceries. She'd impulse-purchased a paperback mystery that she was determined to lose herself in until bedtime.

Timothy had left off one or two lights, but the house still glowed like a party about to happen.

Maxey fed Moe, put away the groceries, checked the dormant answering machine, and was about to open a can of vegetable soup for supper when footsteps echoed up her stairwell.

13

■ ■ ■

''Who is it?'' Maxey called before the knock, and she felt a niggle of disappointment when Timothy's voice answered.

''The bearer of good tidings. Or more like the bearer of good chicken,'' he added as she swung the door open, and he held the red-and-white carton aloft. ''You haven't eaten yet, have you?''

Greasy meat didn't appeal, but she had to be gracious, remembering all the times she'd attempted to cheer up Timothy with food. She swept three days' worth of neglected mail into a pile at the back of the kitchen table and they sat down to eat.

''Man, those stairs could use a landing or two. No wonder you've got a great figure.'' Before Maxey could be embarrassed or take offense, he changed the subject. ''What's the word on Professor Vogle's sister?''

Maxey shook her head. ''No change. She's lucky to be alive, but not if she stays in a coma.''

''Are the cops guarding her, in case the jerk who did it tries again?''

''I guess so. I hope so.'' She forced herself to take a bite of chicken. ''Let's change the subject, huh?''

''Okay. I read today's *Regard* cover to cover. Are you going to let me write some articles?''

''You can try it. What kind of articles do you want to write?''

Timothy opened a catsup packet with his teeth. ''Hard news. Like Reece's story about the kids beating up the vagrant on Iris Street. Or yours about the arson on Nebraska.''

Maxey chewed dutifully. ''You sure you don't want to cover the city council meetings?''

''No, come on. It must be fun to be in on real action, a fire and stuff.''

''Well, yeah. *Interesting* is a better word than *fun*.'' Maxey stood up to get a glass and pour it full of milk. ''Want some? What I like is learning interesting things that don't even show up in the finished article.''

''For instance?''

Maxey, glad that Timothy seemed fully distracted from his own blues, worked enthusiasm into her answer. ''For instance, the fire investigator showed me around that burned house on Nebraska. We even went down in the cellar, and he showed me a thumbprint he's convinced is the arsonist's.''

''No kidding? What on?''

Maxey laughed. "A pickle jar."

Timothy put down the drumstick he'd been worrying and scrubbed at his chin with a napkin, staring at nothing. "Why couldn't there have been a jar of pickles in that VW bus?"

"Timothy—"

"Are you working on my grandmother's killing?"

Maxey set aside her own piece of chicken and pushed back from the table. "You know I am."

"How are you going to have time? I mean, now you have the attack on the Vogle woman to puzzle out, don't you?"

"Maybe it's all one case."

Timothy cocked his head, skeptical. "What makes you think that?"

"It's just too much of a coincidence otherwise. Two women closely connected to the Gunderloy house."

"Yeah, but coincidences do happen."

"Yeah."

"Well, so what do you know so far about what happened to Ms. Vogle?"

Reluctant to add to Timothy's burden of depression, Maxey shook her head.

"Really. I'm interested. Maybe if you give me what you know so far, I can suggest something you haven't thought of." Timothy leaned back in his chair, arms folded.

"She was clubbed on the back of the head with

the proverbial blunt instrument. Then the attacker found a towel somewhere, soaked it in gasoline, wrapped it around her head, and set it on fire.'' Unable to look at the remnants of the chicken anymore, Maxey rose and transferred the entire mess into the kitchen waste can.

''Why?'' Timothy said.

''Why what?''

''Why try to incinerate her like that?''

Maxey sat down again. ''I guess because he hoped the whole house would go up in flames and destroy all the evidence. Except—why the dumb towel on her head? Why not use his gasoline on the dry porch, where there was a better chance of getting a real fire going?''

Timothy jumped up. ''Okay if I have some milk after all?''

She nodded mechanically. ''He must have been trying to destroy evidence of what he thought was the deathblow. He must have thought he could hide the fact she'd been attacked. Or something about the head wound itself might have incriminated him—the angle of attack or the weapon that was used or—what else could it be, Timothy?''

''You're doing fine. Go ahead and dope it out.''

''Dope is probably right. The would-be killer is a dope who doesn't have any clear plan for what he does. Coasting cars into sweet old ladies. Setting puny fires that go out before he's halfway home. He must have a motive, but he sure lacks finesse.''

"Why are we referring to him as 'him'? What happened to equality for women villains?''

"I just don't picture a female doing these weird things, do you?''

"Oh, I don't know, Maxey. I could picture *you* doing them.''

She rewarded him with a laugh before stretching and yawning, hoping he'd take the hint and his leave.

"You want to do something fun for a change this weekend?'' he asked. "Go to a rock concert or spend a day waterskiing or something?''

"Oh, I don't think so, Timothy, but thanks any—''

"Aw, come on. Cheer me up. What would you like to do? How about a hike in the foothills Saturday morning?''

Maxey grinned. "You know what I'd really like to do? Let's take a tour of the Gunderloy house. You have a key, don't you?''

Timothy groaned. "You'd rather hike around an old house than be out in the fresh air?''

"Have you seen it yourself? Don't you want to inspect your property?''

"I was in it once or twice when I was a kid. Not lately though.'' He cleaned off a milk mustache with the back of his hand. "It *was* kind of a neat place to explore. Oh, all right. What time Saturday do you want to run over there?''

''How about after noon sometime? I'll see you at the office tomorrow and we can decide.'' Maxey felt a tickle of anticipation. Timothy's plan for raising spirits was working for hers already.

■

On Friday morning, Maxey sat at her desk preparing tear sheets of Thursday's *Regard* to mail to advertisers along with the bills for their advertisements. When she came to Skye and Skye's full-page spread, she set it aside. If she delivered it in person, she'd have a chance to observe the suspect developer in his natural habitat.

Reece went out for lunch at noon. When he strolled back half an hour later, Maxey snapped a rubber band around two stacks of envelopes that held her morning work, crammed them into her shoulder bag, and swept up the lone envelope to take to Charles Skye.

''I'll be gone for about an hour. If you don't see or hear from me by three, call Sam Russell and tell him I was going to the offices of Skye and Skye.''

''Dang, you sure are paranoid since you became an amateur detective.''

''It's my bad karma. It breeds paranoia.''

''Burnell, I love it when you talk dirty.''

■

Skye and Skye occupied the entire top floor of the Rippler Building, a glass and fieldstone office complex on West Arapahoe Avenue. Maxey stepped out of the hushed elevator into a hushed reception area dominated by one chrome desk shaped like an artist's palette, with a sleek young woman where the thumb should be.

The walls were white; the chairs were white; the receptionist was white. The carpet—white—felt like sponges underfoot. Walking gingerly to the desk, Maxey smiled.

"May I see Mr. Skye?"

The woman had a knack for smiling as if she truly cared. "Which Mr. Skye do you mean?"

"The younger."

"Do you have an appointment?"

"No. But he is expecting this." Maxey held up the envelope with the ad inside.

"I'd be happy to give it to him."

"Thank you, but I'd rather do it myself. It would only take a minute."

The woman reached for her white telephone. "Your name?"

"Maxey Burnell." Doubting that Charles Skye would remember who that was, she added, "From the *Regard.*"

Leaning into the receiver, the woman murmured a

few discreet words. Looking up and activating the smile, she told Maxey to go right in. ''Through that door.''

''That door'' disclosed another monochromatic room, this one in myriad shades of gray—charcoal-and-silver wallpaper in a fleur-de-lis design, fat chairs and a sofa in dove gray corduroy, and slate gray carpeting made of thicker sponges than the one in the reception area. At the far end—which was very far—ceiling-to-floor windows let in a magnificent view of Boulder Creek Path weaving through the greenery of Eben G. Fine Park.

''Ms. Burnell. Do you always provide such personalized service to your advertisers?'' Charles Skye stood up between her and the view and offered a hearty handshake across the expanse of his chrome and glass desk. ''Sit down?''

Since he'd made it a question, she took the hint and remained standing. ''I won't bother you that long.''

''No bother, talking to a pretty lady when I ought to be working.''

''Here's a tear sheet of your ad. Did you see Thursday's *Regard*?''

''Matter of fact, yes. Yes.'' He neither smiled nor frowned to indicate what he thought of it.

''So, did you want to continue with us?''

''You're a little worried about the piece you wrote about the Gunderloy.''

''I'm not worried,'' she said, emphasizing the first word. ''I thought you might be.''

He rested one navy-trousered leg on the edge of the desk and test-touched the knot on his red silk tie. ''Well, Maxey, you did a pretty good job of reporting the facts. Of course, I'm disappointed you didn't present our side as eloquently as you did the historic preservationists' side. But you know, I think readers of the *Regard* are going to be impressed with Skye Developers. They read this none-too-favorable story about us, and then on the very next page, hey, Skye has a big advertisement. And next week, here's another big ad. These Skye guys aren't worried about what a news reporter thinks. They're generous enough to ignore bad press and go on about their business. That shows confidence that what they're doing is right, wouldn't you say?''

''Did you know that Celia Vogle was almost murdered Monday night?''

''Yes, of course. She doesn't like me, but I don't dislike her. I'm sorry it happened.''

''There will be plenty of other preservationists to take her place if she can't continue.''

''I'm sure there will. It may sound odd to you, but this kind of fight invigorates me. It's a part of a developer's job description that I truly enjoy.''

From Skye's desk, a trembling voice rose out of the intercom. ''Charlie, you come in here right now. I'm tired of waiting.''

Skye grinned ruefully at Maxey. "My dad wants to confer." He lowered his voice to a whisper. "It's one of the duties of this job that's less enjoyable."

"Sorry to hold you up," Maxey said, turning to go.

He walked with her into the reception area. "Anytime you want to interview me for a rebuttal, I'm available."

"I'll certainly consider that."

Nodding dismissively, Skye opened the first door to the left of his office. Maxey glimpsed a blue room and a wisp of a man shuffling toward a wet bar the size of Maxey's entire kitchen.

■

She found Timothy alone in the office, typing, two-fingered, at Reece's desk. "Hi. Whatcha doing?" she asked.

"I interviewed Chet Vogle after class this morning, and I'm writing a human-interest story about his sister and him."

"You didn't! He was willing to talk to you about her?"

"Not at first, but he agreed to give me a few comments, and once we got into it, he sort of spilled over. You know? Like he needed to talk about her, to ease the pressure of his worry. Before I got out of his office, I wanted to cry, too, and I don't even know the woman."

Maxey slung her shoulder bag into the bottom drawer of her desk and went to look over Timothy's shoulder.

"Not yet," he exclaimed, using his cast to block out the platen from view. "You don't let people see your rough drafts, do you?"

She kept walking, detouring toward the coffee machine. "Did Chet have any theories about who tried to kill her?"

"A vagrant. She surprised someone who didn't like surprises. This someone thought she'd have money on her, maybe, or wanted to rape her. Probably crazy. He hit her too hard and then panicked."

"Actually, that sounds plausible to me." Sipping coffee, Maxey returned to her desk. She sat down and sifted through the morning's mail: five bills, one check, and a Victoria's Secret catalog with Reece's name on it.

"How about four o'clock tomorrow?" Timothy said.

"How about four o'clock tomorrow what?" She flipped through the catalog, wondering if her life would get better if she bought herself a swimsuit that seemed to be made of four white pot holders.

"The Gunderloy tour you wanted. I've got some stuff to do in the morning, is why I can't do it earlier. If we make it late in the day, we can go somewhere for dinner after."

"Oh, yeah. Four would be fine." She flipped to a

page of underwear and hesitated over the pink floral bra and panties before deciding they'd make her look like a nudist with a rash.

"Grandmother did have a will. The reading is in the morning."

She threw aside the catalog and grimaced at Timothy, who had leaned back in Reece's chair to stretch his right arm.

"But I already know what it says, because the lawyer gave me a preview of coming attractions," he said. "I get everything. If I had died before Grandmother did, all the property would have been sold and the proceeds would have gone to her favorite charities—the public library, arthritis research, and I forgot what all." He grinned. "I'll donate something to each of them anyway, because she would have liked me to."

"Good for you. What about the Gunderloy?"

"I don't know yet. I have to hear what Skye has to say before I make up my mind."

"Don't do anything for a while. Think about it."

"Maxey, don't—"

The telephone rang; he reached to answer Reece's extension, and Maxey turned to her own work.

"Yes, ma'am, we have a circulation of over five thousand, and the lowest classified ad rates in Boulder County," Timothy said.

She smiled before tuning him out to concentrate

on an editorial about the unfair male clique of Catholic priesthood.

■

Friday night. He should have been out at a bar, enjoying himself in a rowdy crowd of strangers. Instead, Tilt sat chain-smoking at the kitchen table, his mind miles away, hearing the seductive invitation of a vacant house.

In the living room, his mother had fallen asleep watching TV. He could see her gray head wobbling on its stalk of neck, her mouth open, her hands limp in her lap—all unaware that her son's addiction to fire was as wide awake as ever.

■

On Saturday, Maxey cleaned house, did the laundry, paid some bills, and looked forward to touring the Gunderloy house.

At five minutes to four, Timothy telephoned.

"It's taking longer to do everything I needed to do. I'll run by and give you the key, and you can start exploring without me. I'll catch up."

"Well . . . okay. Where are you now?"

"North Broadway. Talking things over with an accountant."

"You don't want to run all the way down here to give me the key. You're closer to Nebraska Street.

Why don't you drop the key off with Bailey Marker?''

''Who?''

''Oh. Well, he might not be home, anyway. I can wait till you're free to go with me.''

''You're going to want to look longer than I'll want to. Besides, don't you want to hunt for clues to the attack in the backyard?''

Maxey laughed. ''You've got me pegged pretty well, Waterford.''

''I'll hide the key on the top of the front-door frame. Can you reach it?''

''If you can get it up there, I'll find a way to get it down.''

''See you as soon as I can,'' Timothy promised, and hung up the phone.

Before running downstairs to her Toyota, Maxey packed a gym bag. She included a sweater, a flashlight, her camera, the ubiquitous notebook and pen, and one stainless-steel spray canister of pepper Mace.

14

Nebraska Street dozed, as usual. Apparently no Joshes lived on this particular block.

Parking in front of the Gunderloy, Maxey scooped the gym bag off the passenger seat and stepped out into the looming shade of the foothills. Three squirrels aborted their afternoon activities to race up the nearest tree trunks and twitch their tails at her.

The front walk felt gritty underfoot. Maxey climbed six stone steps to the L-shaped porch that wrapped the front and south sides of the mansion. She eyed the unexpectedly tall front door, doubting that she could jump high enough to reach a key secreted on top of the faded red frame.

Then she laughed, seeing the overturned bushel basket Timothy had left in perfect position. Weathered and dirty, it crackled ominously when she stepped up on it, but it held as long as it took for her to swipe at the grimy wooden ledge and knock the key, clinking, to the floor.

Twisting it in the lock, she let herself into Madame Gunderloy's house.

The vestibule's cherry walls glowed in the late-afternoon light until she shut the door, and then the wood went dim and dull, like a flower past its prime. To the right were stairs. A heavy carved banister soared upward, took a hard right turn, and disappeared. Straight ahead, a wide, high-ceilinged hall led past a shallow fireplace into what must have been the dining room. The kitchen lay visible beyond that. To the left, a huge room, swollen with bay windows that still wore remnants of brocade drapes, beckoned to Maxey.

She went to stand in the center of the bare oak floor, under a faceted glass chandelier that looked like a snarl of necklaces and must have been hell to clean. The parlor: What would it have been like to sit on a horsehair sofa there by the ceramic fireplace, waiting for a man to select you for a trip up those U-turn stairs across the hall? Sort of like taking part in a pickup ball game, worrying you'd be the last team member chosen! But much, much worse once the game got under way.

Maxey strolled into the vacant, echoing dining room and on into the kitchen. She had seen this room before—the no-frills sink, the once-white cupboard, the wire flyswatter on its nail in the curling pink wallpaper. Looking out through the speckled glass window of the door she had once looked in, Maxey could see the black iron fence. An errant strip of yellow police-scene tape clung to it.

Numerous doors riddled the room. Dropping the heavy gym bag in one corner, Maxey snooped behind each door: a pantry lined with cedar shelves and enough dirt on the floor to plant flowers. Another storeroom, where an ancient wringer washer hunkered in the shadows; a butlery full of drawers and overhead cabinets, all empty as far as Maxey checked; a scullery containing another ugly sink and rotting woodwork. The last door that Maxey opened led up steep risers to the second floor.

She climbed, hearing the wind prowl around the chimneys, feeling like a Jane Eyre or a Nancy Drew, with only that glimpse of yellow tape to dampen her enthusiasm for the exploration. She was grateful for the chance to do it alone, the better to soak up the atmosphere.

At the top of the stairs, a narrow hall stretched toward the front of the house. It was lined with doors, most of them closed, like a hotel. She paused to investigate nearly every room, finding all of them barren of furniture, all of them depressing in a way that had nothing to do with the slick of dust that coated them.

The largest room, on the front north corner, opened onto a balcony over the porch roof. Maxey rattled the French doors open and stepped outside. For a moment, she was Fionna Estelle Gunderloy, taking the evening air, perhaps sipping at a shot glass of whiskey, smoking a brown cigarette she'd rolled herself, feeling the breeze as balm to her forehead and neck and cleavage.

The sensation of possession stopped as soon as Maxey returned inside and carefully closed the doors. She glanced at her watch and was amazed to find she'd been poking around for almost an hour. Should she wait for Timothy? Should she go home?

What? And miss the attic and a possible basement?

Retracing her route toward the back stairs, she opened doors that she hadn't tried earlier. One concealed a bathroom big enough for a dormitory, but it contained just one scrawny sink and one oval bathtub that gripped the floor with clawed feet.

The door next to the bathroom led up another flight of precipitous stairs to the third floor. Bracing herself with a hand on either wall, Maxey followed the stairway to a hot, open expanse of attic.

Like the rest of the house, it lay empty of everything except spiderwebs and neglect. Long shadows blotted the raw wood floor. Maxey was drawn to the northwest corner, where dirt-encrusted windows encircled the little witchy-roofed tower. From here, she could see most of Nebraska Street. Her car looked like a plastic model. Timothy's Ford, which would always be Mrs. Waterford's Ford to Maxey, was still not in sight.

When she walked to the other end of the attic, one small wavy-glassed window let Maxey overlook the backyard. Exactly where down there had Celia been standing when the blunt object made its irrevocable difference? Deciding to go outside and look around, Maxey eased down the stair steps, each one too shallow for her whole foot to fit any way except sideways.

She'd left the door at the bottom standing open. Stepping out of the stairwell into the second floor hall, she began to turn around to close the door. A shadow spread across the floor and over her shoes. It moved as her head was swinging around, as her ears were acutely aware of a rustle like stiff cloth against dry skin, as her common sense woke screaming for the gym bag with its Mace, left behind in the kitchen. She felt the air sweeping ahead of the blow, felt the atmospheric compression before the moving solid object, and never felt the blow itself.

■

Tilt ground his cigarette into the black plastic ashtray on his maple nightstand and swung his feet to the floor. He put on his shoes, tested his pockets for handkerchief, wallet, pocketknife, car keys, matches. Easing his bedroom door open just short of where it would squeak, he slipped into the dark hallway. His mother's snores buzzed and died, buzzed and died, as steady as Tilt's heartbeat.

In the kitchen, he eased the dead bolt out of its socket and squeezed out into the night. The hum of distant traffic and the chirp of crickets accompanied his walk from house to garage to car. The engine starting sounded as loud as a cough in church. Once, about halfway to his destination, Tilt braked with too much force, and the cans behind his seat sloshed, their perfume filling him with desire.

■

She was having one of those horrible dreams where she thought she was awake but she couldn't move, couldn't even open her eyes. *Help,* Maxey tried to say, but nothing came out.

Sleep paralysis—she'd read that it was a genetic tendency probably triggered by repression of anger during the day. What had she been angry about?

Celia. Mrs. Waterford. Sam Russell.

The article also said it might simply be a deficiency of potassium in one's diet.

I promise I'll never forget my daily multivitamins again. Wake up, damn it.

The last time she'd experienced sleep paralysis—years ago—she had felt someone watching her, standing behind her, breathing on her. She couldn't cry out to Reece, her husband then. Even if she could have spoken, she wouldn't have shouted for Reece, because she had an unreasonable doubt about whether he cared if she lived or died. Of course, when she finally broke the grip of the nightmare and really wakened, there wasn't a bogeyman in sight. Was that the morning she decided to embark upon divorce?

Is there anyone really here now, or is that rhythmic sighing coming from my own lungs?

Panic wouldn't help. The article she'd read advised that victims of sleep paralysis should move their eyes in quick scanning motions—up, down, left, right—and try to blink. This might lead to freeing of facial muscles and a gradual, systematic release of more distant muscles. She willed her eyes to shimmy like twin Madonnas, but still they didn't bounce open.

Maybe they are open, and I'm blind. Wake up, wake up, wake up, wake—oh God, maybe there's a towel around my head.

■

Tilt swept his car in a U-turn at the barricade and parked in the same place he'd parked a week ago, well away from any streetlamps. He waited five minutes, watching for anyone up and about. Where had his blackmailer been that he'd seen Tilt running from the last fire? And who, damn it? That old man the newspapers said lived in the house next door? Professor Chester Vogle up the street? Did Tilt know anyone except Chet on this street? Not that he was aware of.

He forced himself to sit tight till two o'clock showed on the dashboard. Then he slipped out of the front seat, retrieved the gasoline cans from the back, and hurried across the street to the safety of blacker shadows in the side yard. Moving more slowly on the uneven lawn, Tilt savored this moment of anticipation before he would enter the house and fill it with his seeds of destruction.

■

This time when Maxey regained consciousness, she knew she was awake. She knew her eyes were open in spite of the absolute darkness that filled them. She lay on her stomach, listless, hearing branches scratch against outside walls. Whatever she lay on seemed exceptionally hard and gritty.

She lifted her head no more than an inch, and a giant clawed hand grasped her above the right ear. While the hand squeezed, she tried to crawl out from under it, but she was paralyzed—not from sleep paralysis this time. Flexing her fingers, she felt rope cutting into her wrists.

She intended to groan, but her voice stuck in her throat, well below whatever it was that clogged her mouth. The grainy surface under her cheek smelled of cedar. When she tried to straighten her knees, her feet—also tied—jammed against a wall.

Someone clubbed the side of my head, tied me up, and put me in the pantry of the Gunderloy house.

It cheered her to be able to reason this well in spite of a headache that must measure six on the Richter scale. Still, the mental exercise depleted her energy. Giving up, she drifted into deeper darkness.

■

Tilt had to make three trips from the car to the house because, knowing how big this job would be, he'd brought six cans of gasoline. Having jimmied open the back door, he stepped into the cave of a kitchen.

Pointing his flashlight at the floor, he switched it on and raked it once around the room. It looked like his favorite kind of place—deserted. Shutting off the light, he brought all the gasoline inside. Only after the half dozen cans lined the wall in military precision did Tilt begin the tour he always indulged himself before setting a fire.

First he tried the faucets on the sink—dry—and then he opened what looked like a closet, disclosing a stairwell. He rubbed his hands together in anticipation; his new gardening gloves rasped like sandpaper. As he began to climb the stairs, a sudden wind shuddered the house.

■

Maxey felt the house shake, and even that slightest touch set waves of pain pounding through her head. She clenched her teeth on the gag in her mouth, terrified of being sick and choking to death on her helplessness.

Who? became her mantra. Who hates me this much? Who and why? Timothy is the only one who knew I'd be here. Not Timothy! He didn't kill his grandmother, and he didn't even know Celia. Did he?

The branch that scratched incessantly at the outside wall must surely be scouring a hole in it. The growing wind egged it on.

Anyone could have seen my Toyota with its MAXEY vanity plates parked out front. Chet? Charles Skye or his pit bull dad? Monica or Brent or Gary? Bailey Marker, for God's sake? Or maybe there's a vagrant living in the Gunderloy. A stranger no one has seen—who is walking around upstairs right now . . . if anyone is.

Please, please don't let me sneeze and explode my head.

■

Tilt took his time, enjoying every minute of his walk through the mansion. On the floor of one room, he found a pearl bead, and in the big bathroom, a wire hairpin. He paused several moments to admire an arched stained-glass window, feeling real regret that it was doomed.

Discovering the door to the attic, he smiled as he mounted the stairs. What a great house. He'd been worried about taking on this assignment. Now he wouldn't have missed it for the world.

■

Awareness lapped at Maxey like a rising tide. She hurt a little less each time she wakened, as numbness grew and spread.

I should try to get up. Get free. Get busy. I will . . . in a minute.

Gosh, I wish Sam was here. No, forget Sam. I wish—a humongous glass of tea with enough ice to sink the *Titanic* . . . and a couple dozen aspirin.

In a minute, I'll do something.

■

Tilt prowled down the front stairs and into the bay-windowed room facing the street. He hadn't seen a door leading to the basement yet. Probably one of the doors in the kitchen, he thought, and then a headlight swept across his eyes.

He leapt back as if the light were acid. He waited, heart galloping, for the car to stop and police to rush the porch.

The lights continued their arc, briefly broadsiding his parked Chevy before finishing the U-turn and continuing on up the street the way they'd come. Slumping, Tilt vented his scare in a string of curses. Then he moved on to the next room and the next, glancing around without stopping, bent on finishing what he'd come to do.

Unscrewing the cap from the first can, clamping the flashlight in his mouth to illuminate his way, he poured a line of gasoline around the northern baseboard of the kitchen, into the hall, into the room with the flashy ceiling fixture, the front room, along the bay windows, and here the can ran out.

Striding to the kitchen, he fetched the second can to take up where the first had left off. The liquid gurgled and glugged as he backed along baseboards, room by room, circling the ground floor.

It took longer than ever before, laying down the gasoline in this huge house, like making languorous love to an enormous woman. He laughed when the last trickle of gas overlapped his original starting place. Switching off the flashlight, he stuffed it into his back hip pocket. He tossed the last can at the center of the kitchen, where the other empties formed a miniature hazardous-waste dump.

As he fished into his shirt pocket for matches, Tilt inhaled with appreciation. This new environmentally correct stuff didn't have the richness of the old gasoline, but it still could give a fellow a petroleum buzz.

He fumbled behind himself to locate the porch door's knob. Knees bent, poised to strike the match and run, he caught his breath, listening.

The house creaked. The wind tapped branches

against it. But Tilt didn't hear another groan, and so he decided he had never heard the first one.

He eased the door behind him open a crack and struck one match in a quick, sure stroke away from himself. Before his right hand carried through with the match, to lob it into a corner puddle, before his left hand reached again for the door behind him, Madame Gunderloy's house exploded.

Boards and glass and bits of cupboard and sink catapulted outward, temporarily changing the direction of the wind. What was left of Ronald Ramon Tilton danced in an orgy of flame.

15

■ ■ ■

Sam Russell's pager chirped until he struggled out of sleep to find it on the nightstand and drag it into range of his blurry eyes. Groaning as he recognized the number he needed to call, he rolled over and groped for the telephone before he remembered where he was.

"Where's the goddamn phone?" he asked. The room remained as quiet as if he was alone.

Huffing an annoyed breath, he fumbled with the bedside lamp until it lit. The room sprang up around him, including the cordless telephone on the table on the other side of the bed. Pulling on his shorts, he walked around to that side and sat on the edge of the mattress to make his call.

A familiar voice answered. "Petrelli."

"What do you want, Pete?"

"Sam, there's a two-unit fire in progress at your last attempted homicide scene—on Nebraska Street."

"Nuts."

"Just thought you'd like to know."

"I would—even though I don't. Anything else?"

"We've got a guy who tried to hold up a convenience store with a snake."

Sam's disbelieving laugh shook the bed. "You're shitting me." He scratched his chest and looked around the room for his pants.

"Truth. He tells the cashier to give him the money or he'll sic this serpent on him."

"What kind?"

"Bull snake or something. Not poisonous, turns out."

Standing, Sam circled around to where his clothes made a cloth puddle on the Oriental rug. "So we try him on an unarmed robbery charge?"

"Snake sure didn't have no arms, that's for sure."

Snickering, Sam disconnected and tossed the phone on his pillow, freeing both hands to pull on his socks.

"Wha's going on?" Paula Koski muttered, half-rolling toward Sam and squinting in the light.

"Gotta go, cop. Catch you tomorrow."

Sighing, she burrowed deeper into the covers. "I should run you in on a Three-oh-one."

He thought for a moment. "What's a Three-oh-one?"

"Leaving after colliding, no personal injury."

■

Sam drove slowly up Nebraska, nosing through the milling crowd of looky-lous, to find a parking place across a driveway next door to the burning house. He rolled down his window and studied the scene.

Five fire trucks, an ambulance, a police car, and a fire chief's station wagon jammed at odd angles in the cul-de-sac. Hoses cluttered the lawn. The firemen, in their tan-and-yellow coats, boots, and helmets, strode about, giving the appearance of efficiency in chaos. Shouted orders vied with the roar of the fire.

The Gunderloy pulsed with light and heat, an up-close and personal sun. Flames burst from every first-story window. Black smoke billowed and dipped from the roof. The rear two-thirds of the house had been skinned of its exterior walls, exposing the rooms inside like a huge dollhouse.

After perhaps ten more minutes, the firemen obviously had it tamed. The sound and fury dwindled. Instead of running, men walked. Instead of leaping, the flames crept. Sam opened his door and stepped out into the acrid night air.

Hands in pockets, he strolled toward the activity. At this house immediately east of the Gunderloy, a pair of firemen rolled the hose they'd been using to wet down the roof, a precaution against the fire spreading.

Cutting across lawns, Sam followed the boundary border of trees and bushes, walking toward the rear of the ruined Gunderloy. The fire still gave off enough heat that he raised his arm to shield his face.

Staring at the house, he failed to notice the outstretched legs until they tripped him.

Sam stumbled, found his balance, and backed away a step to check what he'd hit.

Maxey Burnell sat with her back against the base of a hefty tree, her open eyes glittering with the reflection of the blaze.

"Maxey?" He squatted to look into her face. "Hey, Maxey. You okay?"

The eyes slowly closed and opened, butterfly wings undulating. "Sam. Just the man I wanted to see."

"What are you doing here?" He brushed her bangs away from her eyes and her forehead, remembering too late how she hated that. "Are you hurt?"

"I was exploring in the Gunderloy and someone hit me. Like they hit Celia."

"Damn. Back of the head?"

"More on the side—right side."

He leaned across her to examine the damage. Sitting back on his heels, he twisted around to shout for a paramedic.

"Then he tied me up and put me in the pantry."

"Damn! Your hands are tied behind your back? I better not move you to cut you loose. Here, I'll get your feet.'' He dug his pocketknife out and began sawing at the twine he now could see was wrapped around her ankles.

''I worked the gag out while I was lying here,'' she said, looking down her nose at the red bandanna in a loose circle around her neck. ''But nobody could hear me yell for help. I guess I should have rolled out in the open, where someone would have fallen over me sooner.''

''Paramedic,'' Sam shouted again. ''Can we get a medic over here?'' Turning back to Maxey, he finished sawing through the scratchy twine. ''How'd you get out of the house?''

''I think the explosion threw me out.''

Sam rolled his eyes. ''Christ, Maxey, you sure know how to have a good time.''

Hearing running feet, he stood up.

''Wait, Sam. Listen. The reason I wanted to talk to you—''

''What have we got?'' the paramedic asked, dropping to one knee. He wore a blue uniform, carried a black first-aid box, and looked like all of sixteen years old.

''Head injury,'' Sam said. ''May be broken bones, too. Possibly internal injuries.''

''Sam, goddamn it. Listen to me.''

He hunkered down beside her while the medic trotted off to get a stretcher.

''Sam, if I was dead here, what would you do?''

"I'd try not to cry in front of everybody, but then I'd go home and hurt like hell."

"That's not what I mean. I mean professionally—what would you do?"

"What is this, Maxey?"

"You'd secure the scene," she prompted.

"And I'd take photos and then I'd turn you over and take more photos. You want me to go on with this? And then I'd look for some goddamned evidence—"

"There! Even though I'm not dead, I want you to look for evidence."

"I will. While you're lolling around the hospital, I'll be drudging away, searching for clues."

"The clues aren't here; they're on the body."

"Well, maybe, but we can't very well perform an autopsy when the victim's still breathing."

"There's stuff you *can* do, though. Take scrapings from under my nails; check my clothes for fibers or hairs or stains; examine the wound for whatever pattern the weapon left in it."

The paramedic and a buddy arrived with a stretcher, an oxygen canister, and various other tools of the trade. The kid, as Sam couldn't help labeling him, knelt on the other side of Maxey and began to sort out an IV apparatus.

"Don't touch me," Maxey snarled. "I'm not asking for medical treatment. I don't want it until this policeman has collected untainted evidence for an attempted murder case.''

The kid raised an eyebrow at Sam. ''Shock?''

''No doubt. Maxey, I'll go with you to the emergency room. We'll talk about it on the way.''

''Here's a blanket,'' the other medic said, handing it to Sam.

''You shouldn't contaminate me with it,'' Maxey insisted, trying to squirm away.

''Maxey, we can always eliminate the fibers from this blue blanket from any other foreign matter we find on you. You're shivering. Shut up and let us help you.''

The kid had just discovered that the hand he'd planned to insert the IV needle into was caught behind Maxey's back.

''She's tied,'' Sam said.

The kid nodded, unfazed by this latest development. He probably planned to write a book someday. ''I can stick it in her elbow.''

''Stick it in your—''

''Shh, Max, honey, he's trying to help you here.''

''I just want to catch the bastard who did this to me.'' Her bravado deteriorated into a whimper. ''And Celia.''

''Me, too. Me, too.'' He patted her blanketed knee and scooted backward to let the medics work.

''Vacuum out my hair,'' Maxey called. ''Don't let

them disinfect my head till you've taken a swabbing.''

''I know my job,'' he answered, thanking the gods of homicide that his customers usually just lay there and let him do all the work.

■

During the three-minute ride to Boulder Community, the older paramedic managed to cut the binding off Maxey's wrists. She couldn't tell much difference—her hands still felt like deflated balloons on the ends of her limp string arms.

Sam didn't ride along in the ambulance, saying he'd follow in his car, but Maxey wouldn't have wagered good money that he'd do that, either.

The paramedics unloaded her at the emergency room, where two nurses and a young Dr. Freud lookalike replaced her clothes with a hospital gown, cataloging all her scrapes and bruises in the process.

''What hurts?'' Dr. Smetana asked, shining a penlight into each of her eyes.

''It'll save time if I tell you what doesn't hurt.''

He felt her over while the nurses took her blood pressure.

''You'd get a more accurate reading if you wait till he's not fondling me,'' Maxey said. Nobody laughed. Too many malpractice suits had spoiled things for everybody, she thought.

"Did Sam Russell tell you what to do about my head wound?"

"Who's Sam Russell?"

"I thought so. That rat fink."

Smetana gently turned her head and leaned over her, examining the damage. He smelled like peppermint. "We're going to take some X rays, and then we'll see about your head. It's not bleeding."

"When you clean me up, I want the swabs you do it with."

He didn't seem surprised, nor did he answer. He probably hadn't heard her.

She shut her eyes against the harsh ceiling light, feeling very much alone.

■

The X-ray table was hard and cold. The technician took enough pictures to fill an album. Maxey said nothing the entire time, yearning for a half dozen aspirin and a quart of iced water, feeling sorry for herself.

Afterward, one of the nurses wheeled her to a second-story room with two empty beds. When she'd been transferred to the one by the window, Maxey stared up at the mauve predawn sky and worried about how her Toyota would get home.

A different nurse, small and sturdy and mahogany-skinned, came in with a basin and antiseptic. "Now then, let's clean you up a bit, sweetheart."

Right behind her came Sam.

"It's about time," Maxey grumbled before she smiled.

"This gentleman wants to comb your hair," the nurse said, rummaging through the shelves of Maxey's bedside stand. "And then he wants your clothes. Just looking at him, you wouldn't think he was a pervert."

Maxey squinted at the woman's name tag. "Carmen, you and I are going to get along great."

■

Dr. Smetana stopped in to see her on his Sunday-morning rounds. His lime green shirt and gold trousers hinted that the trunk of his car would be full of golf clubs.

"So what all's wrong with me? In twenty words or less."

"Concussion," he said. "Assorted contusions. Three words." He still didn't smile. She'd always imagined that Sigmund Freud had no sense of humor, either.

"When can I go home?"

"Ah, the universal, burning question of every soul ever admitted to any hospital. Give us three or four days. Although there's no skull fracture, a concussion needs time to heal."

"I'm in good shape for being blown up, huh?"

"Last winter, we had a case of an infant whose

parents' gas heater exploded. The baby was found on the next-door neighbor's lawn. Not a scratch on her. You were unconscious when the house exploded?''

''I guess.''

''The baby was probably asleep. The more relaxed you are, the less likely you are to be injured in a collision or an explosion, or whatever.''

''Go with the blow.''

''Yes.''

The sound and scent of breakfast trays being distributed along the hall made Maxey forget about flight plans.

■

Because he was the logical choice, Maxey telephoned Timothy to take care of Moe.

'' 'Lo?''

''Timothy, I need a favor.''

''Who is this?''

''Sorry. Maxey. Timothy, I need a favor.''

''Jeez, just a minute.'' It sounded as if he had dropped the telephone. Seconds later, he said, ''Sorry. What?''

''Did I get you out of bed?'' She looked at her wrist, but the name band on it didn't tell time.

''Yeah. What did you want, Maxey?''

''Moe. Could you please use your key to go up and feed him twice a day for the next couple of days?''

"Yeah. Why?"

"Because I'm in the hospital." She looked around the room, suddenly amazed that she was indeed in Boulder Community Hospital instead of dead. And talking to people instead of being in a coma. She needed to check on Celia while she was here.

"Jeez, Maxey, what happened to you?"

"Where *were* you last night? Why didn't you meet me at the Gunderloy?"

"It took so long at George's—that's the accountant—that I figured you must have finished looking around and gone home."

"Didn't you notice that my car wasn't at home?"

"Mmm, no. I didn't think about it."

She wished she could see him. Was he really sleep-befuddled, or was it panicky surprise at her being alive that addled his wits? "But you'll take care of Moe?"

"Sure. You going to tell me what happened?"

Why should she tell him what he might already know? Giving him the benefit of the doubt, she broke the news that his historic house on Nebraska Street was now history.

■

Maxey wakened from a nightmare involving Buddha statues and stairs running with blood just as Sam Russell strode into the room and thumped a vase of red roses on the rolling table at the foot of the bed.

"You never gave me flowers before."

"I'm not a flower kind of guy."

"You won't be giving me flowers again."

He sat down on the edge of the bed, carefully, so as not to jar her head. "I won't, huh?"

"If this were a soap opera, my nearly getting killed would have showed you how much you . . ." She couldn't say *loved.* She let the sentence die a natural death.

Sam folded his arms and watched her.

"We can always be friends, though, can't we?" Maxey smiled and her whole face ached with the effort.

"Friends," he said, lifting her hand to give it a gentle shake. "How did you know?"

"Mostly it was the pickpocket lie."

"Pickpocket." His brow furrowed. Maxey's hurt just to look at it.

"The night Mrs. Waterford was killed. I asked you what you and Paula were doing at Chautauqua, all dressed up and smelling of beer, and you said you were at the concert on a pickpocket detail. Homicide detectives don't get rinky-dink assignments like that. In fact, I'm not sure anybody gets pickpocket assignments."

Sam laced and unlaced his fingers with hers. "If it's any consolation, I don't expect this thing with Paula to last, either."

"Whatever you're looking for, I hope you find it."

He returned her hand to its resting place on her waist, patted it once, and reached into his shirt pocket for notebook and pen. "Okay, Ms. Burnell, let's get your statement. Did you see who bopped you on the head? Hear his voice? Smell his after-shave?"

"No. None of the above."

"What time did you get to the Gunderloy house?"

"About four-fifteen. Is my Toyota still parked there?"

"No, it's back on Spruce Street. One of my guys hotwired it and drove it home for you. Why were you at the Gunderloy?"

"Because Timothy had agreed to give me a tour of it. He couldn't make it at the time we'd planned, so he left me a key so I could go in and snoop around on my own."

"Who else knew you were there?"

"Nobody. But anyone could have seen my car and figured it out. Listen, I want to thank you for going along with me on collecting evidence from my miserable person. How soon will you know if we got anything useful?"

Sam shook his head. "CBI isn't going to be in any hurry to get back to us on it. We're in line behind a lot of other requests for analysis."

"CBI is—"

"Colorado Bureau of Investigation. They've got the labs and equipment."

They both lapsed into a thoughtful silence until Maxey exclaimed, "Damn. My wallet was in a gym bag in the Gunderloy kitchen. All my credit cards and my driver's license—this killer guy is getting to be a real pain in the ass." She cautiously shifted her hips. "Literally. Sam, you've got to find him."

"We may already have."

"We may? No kidding?"

"Arson investigation turned up a right hand—a man's, we think—in the bushes northeast of the house. They're keeping an eye out for more pieces."

"Ugh." Maxey stared at the speckled tile ceiling beyond Sam's head. "Why didn't he finish me off at five o'clock? Why bother to tie me up and wait all those hours to set a fire?"

"The old 'two birds with one stone' theory. He must have wanted you dead and the Gunderloy destroyed. He couldn't safely instigate arson till it was dark and the neighbors were in bed."

"Maybe three birds, one stone. He committed suicide, didn't he?"

"Any dumb schmuck who plays with gasoline and matches has got to have a death wish, that's for sure."

"I can hardly wait to find out who he was."

■

About twenty-four hours was all she had to wait. Monday morning, after Maxey enjoyed breakfast and a sponge bath, Calen Taylor rapped on the door frame of her room.

"Are you busy?" he asked, waiting for permission to come in.

She adjusted the front of the clean but wrinkled blue hospital gown. "I know it looks as if I'm just lying here, but actually I'm actively engaged in getting better. I can do two things at once, so please sit down and talk to me. How nice of you to come."

He walked into the room and pulled the visitor's chair closer to the bed. His off-duty attire consisted of blue jeans, white sneakers, and a bright green polo shirt.

He settled into the chair, elbows on the armrests, hands clasped across his stomach. "I'm glad I'm visiting you here instead of at the funeral parlor."

"Amen. Tell me what you know about the Gunderloy arson."

"The same person set it who set the one across the street."

"Don't tell me. You matched the hand in the bush with the prints on the pickle jar."

"Once in a while, we get a break." He smiled and touched his mustache. "Motor vehicles did a search on the plates on his Chevy, which was parked across the street, and we ran a check on the name. Ronald Ramon Tilton. He'd been incarcerated for arson two years ago."

Maxey shook her head. "I don't know him. Was he homeless? Camping at the Gunderloy?"

"No. Living with his mother here in town somewhere."

"Did he try to kill Celia?"

Calen shrugged. "No evidence in that direction."

No, and Maxey didn't think Tilton had tried to kill *her* either.

"Are you married?"

"Excuse me?"

"I need someone to celebrate with me, when I get out of here."

"Divorced."

"Good. I mean—"

"I accept the invitation."

16

■ ■ ■

After Calen left, Maxey napped. Every few minutes, a voice in the hall, or a nurse performing some ritual in her room, or the persistent ache in her head would dredge her up from the bottom of sleep. Then almost immediately, she'd sink back into unconsciousness.

She shook off lethargy long enough to enjoy everything on a crowded lunch tray. Not an aficionado of afternoon TV, she wished for something to read, but when a gift shop volunteer came around with a trolley of supplies, including magazines and newspapers, Maxey found that scanning one section of the *Denver Post* was enough to make her eyes and arms ache.

She wakened from another nap, to find the room beginning to dim and Reece sitting in the visitor's chair reading her *Post.* The three pink balloons that seemed to be growing from his head were really part of a floral arrangement sitting on the radiator cover behind him.

"Did you bring flowers, Reece? Thanks if you did, and shame on you if you didn't."

"Ah, she's not dead, only sleeping," he said, tossing the paper on the foot of the bed. "How do you feel?"

"Like an elephant stepped on me. Did you miss me today?"

"You weren't at work? No kidding? I suppose you're going to claim you can't open the office in the morning either."

"You want a written excuse from my doctor?"

Reece was wearing a red muscle shirt that he'd probably made himself from an old sweatshirt, using a pair of dull scissors. His cutoff blue jeans dripped long threads that must have tickled his tanned thighs. He slung one knee casually over the arm of the chair and leaned back, at home and in no hurry. "Bet I know something you don't know."

"You might know one thing. Everything else I know just as well as you do." Smiling still made her face feel like ice cracking in all directions.

"The guy who set the Gunderloy fire was a student in one of Chet Vogle's classes."

She shut her eyes to think about it. "The two knew each other, huh? Did what's his name—Tilton—know Celia, too?"

“That would be more than one thing. You conceded I'd know only one thing.”

“Oh. Right. How'd you know that one thing?”

“Timothy told me. He's in the same class—the care and feeding of fantastic fantasy writers or some such elective profundity. Timothy's volunteered to skip the class, by the way, and help me run the office full-time till you get back. Says old Chet isn't teaching worth a damn right now anyway, so he won't be missing anything.”

Maxey inched a little higher on the pillows. “Reece, you're just about the only person I don't suspect of clobbering me. Who do you think did it?”

He considered, brushing his jawline with the knuckles of one hand. “I'd have to say Timothy Waterford.”

Depression dropped over her like a weighted net. “Why?”

“So he'd have an excuse to cut classes and scarf all the M & M's you've got stashed in your middle desk drawer.”

“No, seriously.”

“Seriously, I haven't got a clue to who or why. Do you?”

“I hope so,” she said, thinking of several brown paper evidence bags with her name on them sitting in someone's in-tray at the Colorado Bureau of Investigation.

■

Maxey didn't worry that the killer would come after her in the hospital. Her room was almost across the hall from a nurses' station, with its constant coming and going of staff. Late Monday evening, another young woman arrived to occupy the second bed, an automobile-accident victim with a swollen face, a broken leg, and enough attentive relatives to scare off any villain bent on sneaking past that bed to Maxey's window location.

Tuesday morning, she ate breakfast, picturing a grumpy Reece arriving at the *Regard* office about five minutes late, Timothy waiting for him on a shady bench in the mall median. The two of them would go inside and, first things first, brew coffee not as good as the cup she now lifted to her lips.

Her friend Carmen came bustling in with a blood-pressure cuff. Maxey suspected that her pleasure at seeing the nurse had less to do with personality than it did with Carmen's having dispensed the painkillers on that first restless night.

"Dr. Smetana says to get you up today. Don't try it by yourself," Carmen said, squeezing the bulb of the apparatus and letting it hiss in release. "He says if you still want to go home, and if you do okay on your feet, you can check out tomorrow."

"Not today, huh?" Maxey reached for a triangle of golden toast to anoint with a smear of apple jelly.

She didn't really want to go home today, not when she could loll around in bed and anticipate two more meals instead.

After breakfast, while Carmen hovered within arms' reach, ready to break her fall, Maxey sat up on the edge of the bed and prepared to stand on her own two feet again.

"Wait a minute. Don't you have any slippers? Stay right there. I'll get you some hospital scuffs."

"I don't have any clothes period," Maxey said to Carmen's disappearing back. Sam had taken all of her Saturday clothes as evidence.

The kelly green slippers that Carmen brought back looked like elasticized refrigerator-dish covers and felt like clown shoes. Maxey would have to phone a friend to bring her going-home clothes. She certainly wouldn't want to be seen in public in whatever hospital outfit matched this footwear.

A few minutes later, having successfully completed the round-trip to the tiny adjoining rest room, Maxey sat on the side of the bed and telephoned the office. She stuck a forefinger in her free ear to muffle the commotion around the other bed, where the accident victim's parents and four other assorted relatives seemed to be planning somebody's wedding.

"*The Blatant Regard,*" Timothy answered, in a voice that was deeper than normal, like a kid playing grown-up. "How may I help you?"

''You sound good,'' Maxey said. ''How's it going?''

''Maxey? We're doing fine. Reece is letting me write a bunch of articles for this week's edition. He says now that I've got some money, I ought to buy out his share of the business.''

''He's been threatening to sell his share since the day he inherited it. He'll be threatening to sell his share when he's ninety years old and recycling all of his old editorials for the umpteenth time.'' At least, Maxey hoped so. ''Timothy, I hate to bother you with this, but, like I said before, you're the one who's got a key to my place.''

''Sure. What do you need?''

''I get to move home tomorrow. I could order a cab, but I don't have any clothes, and I don't want to be delivered to the police station for indecent exposure.''

Timothy said it would be no problem. They set a time. Maxey thanked him and disconnected. She eased back into bed, as winded as if she'd been sprinting in the halls.

■

Maxey lay with her arm across her eyes, wondering what her attempted murderer was doing right now.

''Maybe she's asleep,'' a feminine voice murmured.

Lifting her arm, Maxey blinked at Monica and

Brent, who were standing irresolutely at the foot of the other bed. Her roommate and entourage had at least temporarily vacated the premises, and the waning afternoon lay in shadows around the quiet room.

"Hi, guys." Maxey straightened the thin cotton hospital gown and ran fingers through her untamed hair, probably making it worse. She'd heard it was a good sign when a patient began to worry about appearance.

"We don't want to bother you," Monica said.

"I'm glad to see you. Sit down and tell me what's going on in the real world."

They were dressed in their white-collar clothes—suits, ties, all buttons buttoned, their own hair.

Brent hauled a chair from the other side of the room, and they sat down opposite Maxey's knees. She felt like a piano about to be played.

"We just looked in on Celia," Monica said.

"How is she?"

"Holding her own."

"Do the doctors think there's brain damage? Is that why she doesn't wake up?"

Brent scooted low in his chair and planted one ankle on the other knee. "According to Chet, all the tests are inconclusive."

"Maybe by the time her burns are healed . . ." Monica's eyes welled with tears that she brushed away impatiently.

"How's Chet holding up?" Maxey pictured his

dour face, always looking as if he'd lost his best friend. Maybe now he had.

"Old Chet's got problems." Brent didn't look too sorry about it.

"He's in jail," Monica said. "Unless his lawyer's bailed him out by now."

"Jail!"

"For assault."

Maxey's hand lifted involuntarily to touch her bandaged head.

"We two and Gary had gone to see Chet, to ask if there was anything we could do, and he tried to brain Gary with a golf club," Brent said.

Monica shifted impatiently in her chair. "Well, Chet was under the influence. He's been drinking way too much lately."

"A golf club?" Maxey marveled. "Why was he that mad at Gary?"

"Chet's convinced himself that Gary did that to Celia," Monica said. "Because Chet saw Gary, so he claimed, in the side yard of the Gunderloy house on the evening she was hurt."

Maxey frowned doubtfully. "I thought Chet was at a travelogue."

"This was before," Monica said. "Supposedly. While Chet was dithering about whether to go on to the lecture without Celia. He says he looked out the front door and saw Gary hurrying toward the back of the Gunderloy. He didn't see Celia though."

Maxey rubbed at her forehead. ''What do you think? Could he have recognized Gary from that far away?''

''Who knows?'' Brent scoffed. ''If he had his usual snootful, he could've recognized the entire Nuggets basketball team in a pitch-black closet.''

''Does Gary have an alibi for that evening?''

''I guess not, but Maxey, he wasn't there,'' Monica said. ''He wouldn't have hurt Celia. Chet's never liked him. Or Brent and me, either, for that matter. If Chet had really seen anything, he would have told the police as soon as they—you—found Celia. Don't you think?''

''I guess. Unless he wasn't sure because, as you say, he'd been drinking. Or maybe Chet attacked Celia himself and he's trying to frame Gary.'' Belatedly, Maxey asked, ''Is Gary okay?''

''Yeah,'' Brent said. ''Chet missed him by a mile. The follow-through sent Chet flying across the dining room. He dug a nice divot out of the tabletop before he could help himself.'' Brent grinned, remembering. ''Gary discreetly took his leave, went to the nearest pay phone, and called nine-one-one.''

''But, Maxey, how are you feeling?'' Monica asked. ''You've got good color in your face.''

''Right,'' Brent said. ''A nice green, a rich purple—sort of a Black Watch plaid.''

Maxey laughed. ''I felt pretty good, till you two started cheering me up.''

"Can we go yet, Monica? Have we done our duty?"

"He hates hospitals. They make him sick." Monica patted Brent's ankle.

Not for the first time, Maxey wondered if they were more than friends. "Are you two more than friends?" she asked.

"Wha—rude? Is this woman a reporter or what?" Brent pretended outrage.

Monica overrode him. "We're very good friends. Platonic."

"What's platonic mean?" Brent pretended to ask behind an open hand.

Monica sniffed. "It means I could never go to bed with a man with a tiny vocabulary."

"What's the size of his vo—"

"Okay, okay, we'll go." She stood and moved the chair back to the wall. "He'll make some woman a wonderful husband when he grows up."

"Thank you for coming by. Stay in touch," Maxey said, offering her hand to Monica. Brent swooped in to kiss it.

After the room settled into quiet, Maxey thought about Chet and Gary. The screws and scoring lines of a golf club's face would surely leave distinctive marks on a victim's head, marks the murderer might try to eradicate with arson.

■

On Wednesday, at about ten o'clock in the morning, a nurse's aide pushed Maxey to the hospital entrance in a wheelchair, to meet Timothy in Mrs. Waterford's Ford. Maxey held Sam's and Reece's flowers on her lap, peering over the tops of the roses, feeling like a hunter in a blind.

Timothy came around to open the passenger door and help her in. His rough cast scraped her elbow, bare below the yellow T-shirt he'd brought for her to wear. He'd also dredged up a pair of bell-bottoms—blue-and-white ticking—from the farthest reaches of her closet. She would have sworn she'd thrown them away in 1979. To complete the ensemble, Timothy had brought her favorite pair of white tennis shoes and no underwear.

"I appreciate you doing this," Maxey said, having to lean back and rest after a brief struggle with the seat belt. The overcast sky stretched above the city like a tattletale gray sheet.

"No problem. I owed you. Also, you needed milk and some other stuff, so I stocked you up. I can bring you a pizza or something for supper tonight."

"You don't need to do that. How much do I owe you for the groceries?"

"Naw, forget it. I can afford it now. I'm thinking of trading this old junker in on a Bronco or maybe a Jag. What do you think?"

She thought he ought to salt it away for his continuing education, but she doubted that saying so would make one speck of difference.

''Do you know how Professor Vogle's sister is doing?'' Timothy asked, speeding up through a stale yellow light, giving Maxey a momentary flashback of a black van missing her by inches.

''I went to see Celia this morning. She's out of intensive care. Now she's got a private room in the burn ward. Most of the damage is to the back of her head. They've shaved what hair she had left. She looks like a prison camp survivor.''

Timothy grunted. ''If she's going to come out of it, wouldn't she have done it by now?''

''I don't think doctors know much about comas. It's just wait, wait, and keep the faith. She could open her eyes this afternoon, or twenty years from now, or never.''

''Even if she wakes up, is she going to be—you know—all right?''

Unable to answer this, Maxey started to shake her head. The motion reminded her of her own injury, and she grieved for Celia all the more.

''Let's change the subject, Timothy. Tell me why you want a Bronco or a Jaguar.''

Happy to oblige, he rattled off prices, features, and trade-in values the rest of the way home.

The house on Spruce Street looked wonderful to Maxey, serene as a vacant ship docked at port. Timothy made a show of running around to help her out of the car, and she let him link arms with her for a slower-than-necessary ascent of the few porch steps.

"Thank you again," she said while he unlocked her front door with his key.

"I'll see you upstairs."

"Oh, I can make it." She stepped into the dim stairwell and looked up at the door to her living room, so near and yet so far. She could always sit down on a step to rest. "Oh, hey, I don't have any keys, Timothy. They probably got exploded to smithereens. Could I have yours?"

"Sure, I've got an extra set." He bear-hugged her shoulders and urged her upward.

The fourth riser squeaked, right on schedule. Moe called from behind the door at the top, cheering her on. The climb seemed interminable.

Three fourths of the way up, Timothy's grip loosened, tightened, and crowded Maxey into the wall. He let go of her and stumbled to one knee on the next step. Maxey clung to the banister, sweating.

"Sorry." He panted. "I misstepped. You should hit your landlord up for an elevator."

Before he could grip her again, she clambered up the last few steps and leaned against the door, waiting for his key. Moe was howling now, a hopeless, mourning declaration that he had never expected to see his roommate again.

Timothy reached the landing, fumbled the key into the lock, and swung the door aside for Maxey. She made it as far as the couch before her legs gave way. Moe stalked over to leap up and patrol the length of the backrest, describing his last lonely days.

"I missed you, too," Maxey said. She wanted to pull him into her lap, but the effort was too great. "You can just leave the key on the counter there, Timothy."

"I'll check on you in a few hours."

"No, don't bother. I'm going to sleep for at least a week."

"Well . . . if you're sure I can't do anything."

"I'm sure." She slid down sideways in the couch and lifted her feet up, shutting her eyes.

After a moment, the door snicked shut. Eyelids squeezed tight, she felt a spasm of irrational fear that if she opened them, Timothy would still be standing there, smiling at her.

Unable to stand the suspense, she snapped both eyes wide and jerked backward from Moe's furry face, inches from her own. Timothy was gone.

Why is it that when I tried to help him after his injury, it seemed like the benevolent thing to do, but when he tries to do the same for me, it feels like an intrusion? No wonder he was so surly and turned away all my efforts; that's exactly what I want to do now.

Fat Moe bounded lightly to the cushion next to Maxey's head and bent to scrub his forehead on her chin. She scratched his ears.

Of course, when I was trying to help Timothy, he didn't have a sneaking suspicion that I'd tried to kill him.

Waiting till Moe lost interest in cuddling, Maxey forced herself up to walk to the phone and call a locksmith for an emergency installation of new locks.

■

For a week, nothing happened.

Maxey, realizing this was probably the first and last vacation she'd get for a while, stayed home, phoning the office once a day to be sure that Reece was awake at the helm.

Timothy, to her surprise and relief, didn't knock at her door every night. When, in fact, he didn't knock at all, she felt a perverse disappointment that he wasn't concerned about her.

The *Camera* printed a two-page pictorial spread about the Gunderloy mansion, before and after. Now that the fine old house had become a charred skeleton, public opinion overwhelmingly supported and missed it. In hindsight, everyone seemed to be a preservationist.

She didn't phone Sam. He would call her whenever he received the report from the CBI lab. There wasn't anything else to discuss with him.

She didn't phone Calen, not willing to risk anything until her previous losses had lost their edge.

Maxey lay low, letting everything heal—head, heart, and all.

On Saturday, she made the mistake of taking a thinking-of-you planter to Chet Vogle.

17

Maxey didn't telephone first to check whether Chet was at home. She rather hoped he wouldn't be, so that she could leave her cheer-up offering on the front porch without having to speak to the man—who wouldn't want either her gift or her gab. The gesture was really for Celia, anyway.

She stopped at Safeway for a glazed pot erupting in pothos, miniature palm, and grape ivy. It all looked green and optimistic now, but she knew from experience that the ivy leaves would turn brown and drop off within a month—if Chet didn't neglect the whole arrangement to death before then.

Parking in front of the Vogle house, she left the planter on the passenger seat and strolled west to look at the Gunderloy place.

Except for rubble, little of the house remained. Two porch pillars and a window frame stood up like tombstones in a battlefield strewn with blackened boards, broken glass, and twisted pipes and wires.

The front steps led to nowhere. The salmon-colored entrance door lay in splinters in the matted grass. All of the closest trees cowered, scorched and leafless. There wasn't a squirrel in sight.

A temporary orange slatted fence had been strung around the ruin. Maxey made a circuit of the house, staying outside the flimsy barrier even though she could have stepped over it in a couple of places where someone else already had.

At the far southeast corner of the foundation, she stopped to gaze at a tattered patch of pink wallpaper on the remains of an interior wall. How long would it have taken Calen to discover her body if the Gunderloy had not spat her out that night?

Shivering in the hot sunshine, Maxey turned to leave. She gasped. Timothy stood watching her, ten feet away. His white shirt and shorts still bore creases from the manufacturer's packaging.

"What's a nice girl like you doing in a dump like this?" he said, sidling closer. He cradled his bad left arm in the crook of his right.

"It's a shame, isn't it?" Maxey looked back at the house. "What are you going to do with it now?"

"Sell it to Skye and Skye and let them worry about it."

"I wish you'd talk to the neighborhood group first. They don't want a condo here. You don't want to do something you'll be sorry for later."

"Well . . . maybe."

Across Timothy's shoulder, Maxey saw someone else striding toward them across Nebraska Street.

"How's the old skull, Maxey?" Timothy tilted his own head, studying her. "You look pretty good."

"I feel pretty good. I'll be back to work Monday."

"Did you see the *Regard* Reece and I put out this week? Not too shabby, huh?" He smiled with obvious pride.

"Yeah, I saw it. That's why I'll be back. Before you guys decide I'm expendable."

The approaching figure resolved itself into Chet Vogle. He reached the Gunderloy yard, scarcely breaking stride to kick at the front tire of the bicycle that Timothy, apparently, had left lying in the grass. Maxey's sense of unease grew as she noticed the odd way Chet walked, swinging one arm while the other seemed caught behind his back.

"Hello," she called with false heartiness. "I was just on my way to see you."

"Don't I have enough troubles?" Chet answered. If he had been someone else, she'd have laughed at his droll putdown. Since he was Chet, her apprehension tightened another notch.

He stopped abruptly and scowled at Timothy. "I know you."

"Yes, sir. I'm a student of yours. Tim—"

Chet's hidden hand whipped around, and the fireplace poker in it swished purposefully at Timothy's head.

"Jesus!" Timothy threw a protective arm in front of his face. The point of the poker chunked against the cast and stuck, like an ax embedded in soft wood.

Timothy staggered backward. The poker, pulled out of Chet's grip, dangled from the cast for a moment before dropping to the grass between the men.

"Chet!" Maxey yelled when he moved to scoop it up again.

Grunting, Timothy stamped a foot on the head of the poker and shifted all his weight to anchor it on the ground. Chet backed away and wiped his palms up and down his shirtfront.

"Chet," Maxey said more quietly. "What do you think you're doing?"

He turned a look of mild surprise on her. "This man almost killed my sister."

In her peripheral vision, Maxey could see Timothy's full-moon face gleaming under a sheen of sweat. He muttered hoarsely, "I didn't."

Maxey studied Chet for signs of inebriation. He stood straight and steady. His eyes met hers in a steady, knowing stare.

He spoke with clipped precision. "This yahoo was going to take her away from me. He didn't want her. He just wanted our money. Well, dreadfully sorry, but I'll require all of it myself. I'm being disemployed by the university, you know."

Timothy, breathing hard, shook his head. "You're crazy. I don't even know your sister."

"I saw you right here that night she nearly died," Chet said, his eyes blank with remembering, "I imagine Celia advised you then that she was no longer infatuated with you. And you lost your temper and you seized a rock and you hit her, and you hit her, and you hit her." Chet's voice thickened with approaching tears. His hands flew up to cover his face. "And now she's not Celia anymore."

Maxey held still as stone, thoroughly convinced by Chet's emotion, afraid to do or say anything that would prompt Timothy to grab up the poker and begin swinging at them.

"Old man, you are crazy," Timothy said, low and venomous. "Just who the hell do you think I am?"

Chet's hands fell away from his eyes and hovered, trembling, at his cheeks. He squinted at Timothy. "Aren't you Gary Prescott?"

Timothy snorted.

"No, Chet, you're confused," Maxey said, stepping closer to take his hands and pull them gently down, leaning in to breathe his scent. Liquor, though faint, was predominant. "You've had too much to drink again."

Timothy bent over and snatched up the poker. "I'm going to sue you into the next county, Vogle."

Chet ripped his hands away from Maxey's and backed out of reach of the poker, as well. "I apologize. You're correct. I am confused. I just don't want to face the verity of the matter." He sighed and squared his shoulders. "I never meant to kill anyone except Leland Pharr. He'd dismissed me, you see. I certainly never meant to kill my poor sister."

Maxey and Timothy exchanged uneasy glances.

"Are you saying you did attack Celia?" Maxey asked.

A mourning dove had time to repeat his four-note eulogy twice before Chet answered. "She was going away. I lost my job, and I wasn't about to lose Celia."

"But by killing her you'd lose her. Forever," Maxey protested.

Chet laid a finger beside his nose, a thin, dour Santa Claus. "There's a difference between being left and being the leaver."

"You go find a phone, Maxey. I'll keep him talking," Timothy murmured.

"No. You go. If he decides you're Gary again, he's liable to launch a fresh assault."

"Maxey, I don't think that's a good idea. Even if I leave you the poker, he could take it away and—"

"Timothy, I'm your boss. Simon says, Go across the street to that white frame house and ask Bailey Marker to use his phone."

While they argued, Chet wedged his fists into his pants pockets and began walking home.

Maxey and Timothy followed. At Bailey's front

walk, Maxey gave Timothy a little push and nodded. He shrugged, handed her the poker, and marched toward Bailey's porch.

Maxey ran to catch up to Chet. Using the poker as a walking stick, swinging it high every other step, she said, "Chet, did you really try to kill Celia?"

"I'm afraid I did."

"You're afraid you did? Or you did?"

"I want to confess my sins, Miss er . . . You needn't try to obfuscate the exegesis."

"What was your weapon?"

"No comment."

"Did you hit me and tie me up? Did you know Ronald Tilton was going to set the place on fire?"

"Your questions are giving me a gargantuan headache."

"Well, you gave me one that lasted a week! You owe me an explanation."

"All you need to know is that I'm riddled with guilt—guilt, 'the avenging fiend, that follows us behind with whips and stings.' "

Stopping, Maxey pointed the poker across Chet's chest, barring his way. "Did you do those things to me? Hit me and leave me to burn?" she snarled.

"Yes."

"Why?"

"I'm sorry, Ms. Burnell. I don't like you."

She lowered the poker and Chet began to walk again.

"And what about Mrs. Waterford?" Maxey persisted.

"Who?"

"The harmless old lady on Baseline. The one hit by a VW bus. Did you do that?"

"Why would I do that?"

Maxey didn't want to lead her witness. "Weren't there other people at the scene that night?" she suggested cautiously.

"That's right. Now I recollect. My intention was to run Leland Pharr down. She must have jumped into my way. That's exactly the kind of disappointment that's been dogging my every moment lately."

Maxey drew a ragged breath and let it out slowly. They had reached Chet's front walk. She stopped and watched him stalk to the porch and into the house. He didn't move as if he'd had too much to drink. Timothy could be right about Chet being crazy.

After a minute of nothing happening, Maxey strolled to Chet's porch, sat on the cement steps with the poker across her knees, and listened through the rejoicing of the neighborhood birds for the wail of an approaching police car.

After a few more minutes, the house that loomed behind her shuddered with one sharp, irrevocable report.

■

Maxey and Timothy sat cross-legged on the grass under an oak tree in the Vogles' front yard, waiting for the police to come out of the house and tell them they could go home.

"I can't believe you didn't go in and look at him after you heard the shot," Timothy said, snapping off a dandelion and twirling it between thumb and finger. "A crack reporter like you. A Komodo dragon detective like you. A good Samaritan like you, who'd worry about whether she could help him."

"Oh, shut up," Maxey said without heat. "Would you have gone in, knowing Chet had a gun? Anyway, I saw a shooting victim once, and once was more than sufficient. Since the police were already on their way, it was easy to sit tight."

Timothy's whole attention seemed riveted on the beautiful weed in his hand. "So he told you he murdered my grandmother?"

"Yes. He didn't mean to hurt her. It was Dr. Pharr he was after."

"Who was the Gary that Chet had me confused with? Do I really look like him?"

"A friend of Celia's, and no, you don't." Maxey studied him, one eye shut. "You've lost some weight."

He sat straighter and patted his belly. "A pound a day for a week. Haven't felt like eating."

"Maybe you do look a little like Gary, bodywise. He's stocky, about your height. Dark hair, too. He models for romance-novel covers,'' she added with a grin, anticipating Timothy's reaction.

''And I look like him? All right!''

A plump policewoman came outside, picked up a satchel from the porch, and reentered the house. The neighbors, all adults and too polite to stand on the curb and gawk, had found excuses to be out in their own yards—watering, weeding, washing their cars. Even Bailey Marker had stationed himself on his front porch in a yellow metal chair facing toward the excitement.

''We can get on with our lives now,'' Timothy said. ''You can stop looking for a murderer behind every bush, and I can start having fun again. I'm going to buy a car, and maybe a new stereo. I'm not sure if I'll stay on Spruce Street or rent that out and find myself a house with more of a view.''

Timothy talked on, his voice and face more animated with every new acquisition he planned to make. Maxey shook an ant off her hand and thought about phoning Calen to claim the dinner date he'd accepted.

Another police car muttered up the street and parked behind the other two. Sam Russell got out, his gray jacket flipping open briefly and revealing the pistol holstered below his shoulder.

''Hello,'' he said, sauntering toward them, stopping to smile down at Maxey. ''We've got to stop meeting like this.''

"Have you got any statements for the press?"

"Word is, he swallowed a twenty-two-caliber bullet from a little Beretta registered to him. Word is, he confessed to you, Ms. Burnell, first. You have a gift for tying up a case all neat and tidy."

"I'd have applied to the police academy instead of journalism school, but I hate push-ups. Listen, Sam, didn't Chet give any indication he had murder on his conscience when you guys took him into custody for trying to birdie Gary Prescott?"

"The man was a mess. After he sobered up, he spoke as rationally as you or I. More rationally than you sometimes." Sam nudged the toe of her sneaker with the toe of his loafer.

Maxey managed to stifle a demeaning desire to throw her arms around his leg and hang on for dear life. Instead, she batted at a sweat bee becoming over familiar with her chin, hoping that Celia didn't know who hit her.

When the police gave them permission to leave, Maxey offered Timothy a ride home, but his bike was too big for her Toyota. As she made the right-hand turn onto Broadway, she saw him in the rear-view mirror, pedaling half a block behind, his white shorts and shirt looking vaguely Oriental, his cast like a loaf of bread across his lap.

■

Night settled over Boulder. One by one, streetlights bloomed. The sounds of children at play faded and winked out. Desultory traffic whispered under Maxey's front windows.

She sat in the soothing twilight of her unlit living room, stroking Moe's furry, bony head, his hot weight across her lap pinning her to the couch.

"I don't know about you," she murmured, "but I've had enough excitement for a while. If you've got anything to tell me, better make it soon, because my brain feels like a breaker switch is about to pop."

Bam! She started, scaring Moe out of her embrace, as the sound of the slamming street door funneled up the entrance stairwell. Footsteps thudded toward the landing in front of her door.

"Damn. Now what?" She reached to switch on the end-table lamp, and her living room leapt up around her in all its cozy but scruffy glory.

Moe, tail twitching, paced to the front door and stared at it till their visitor knocked. "Hey, Maxey?"

She tried to keep annoyance out of her voice. "What do you want, Timothy?"

"I brought you a present."

"What for?"

"I didn't get you flowers or anything when you were in the hospital. I keep forgetting I've got the money now to do nice things like that. Wait. You don't have to get up. I've got my key."

She rushed to open the door before he could try to

insert it, feeling vaguely guilty for having changed the lock.

Timothy stood grinning in anticipation of her reaction to the silver-and-white-striped package he proffered her. It had the unmistakable heft and shape of a hardback book.

Backing into the living room, she slid one finger under the adhesive tape. ''This better not be something too expensive, Timothy. You may have money now, but pretty soon you won't have if you—''

Timothy's self-satisfied smile grew as her mouth dropped. The book, green with decay, smelling of mold, came into the light from its fancy wrapper like a disinterred corpse. No title or author interrupted the austere black cover.

Maxey cautiously opened it near the front. Spidery brown handwriting, left-leaning and full of ornate loops, sprawled across the pages.

Timothy couldn't wait any longer to enlighten her. ''It's Madame Gunderloy's diary. I found it along with a bunch of other old books in Grandmother's bookcase. She must have discovered it at the house.''

''You can't give it to me. It's yours.''

''It doesn't mean that much to me. I don't want it. I knew you would, though.''

''I would. I do.'' Impulsively, she stretched out her arm and hooked him close enough to kiss his cheek.

''I'm glad the arsonist didn't get you,'' Timothy

said, his eyes gleaming with real emotion as he patted her shoulder.

The telephone rang.

"Excuse me," Maxey said. Although she could have let the answering machine handle it, the interruption was just what she needed to arrest her slide into sentimentality. "Hello?" She held the diary against her chest, grinning at Timothy.

"Maxey," Sam's gruff voice filled her ear. "I just found the CBI report on my desk."

"Oh, great. Now that we have the case all wrapped up." Carrying the receiver to the couch, she sat down and tucked her legs under her. "So did they find any corroborating evidence? Did my body yield any clues?" She winked at Timothy, who didn't seem to notice he was staring and avidly eavesdropping.

"Maxey, the combings from your hair—there were traces of fiberglass in it."

"Fiberglass," Maxey blurted before she could bite her tongue. She frowned down at Moe on the floor, grooming himself with one hind leg straight up in the air, and she felt Timothy's stare boring into her forehead.

Sam continued to talk about the swabbing from her wound yielding fiberglass dust and one flake the size of a pinhead. Maxey continued to watch Moe as if she'd never seen a feline contortionist before.

"So, unless you had a run-in with a fiberglass curtain earlier that day,'' Sam said, ''I think you can see where this points.''

''Yes. I understand.'' Taking one fortifying breath, she looked up at Timothy and smiled a wide, artificial smile. ''He's here with me right now, Sam.''

''I'm on my way,'' Sam snarled, and the telephone went as dead as Timothy Waterford's eyes.

18

■ ■ ■

The cream-colored cast on Timothy's left forearm and hand drew Maxey's eyes the way a sleeping rattlesnake would do—unwillingly, as if seeing it clearly might instigate its attack. He held it against his stomach, his exposed fingers like pale sausages poking out the end. An ugly depression in the fiberglass marked where Chet had punctured it with the poker.

"You ought to have a doctor check that," Maxey said, nodding. "It could have bent the cast out of shape against your arm."

He shrugged. "It doesn't hurt. It's amazing how hard it is." He turned toward the counter that divided kitchen and living room, and, screaming like a Ninja, he smacked the flat of the cast against the countertop.

"Ohmygod," Maxey said, backing deeper into the couch. Moe leapt sideways, his tail a bottlebrush, and skittered into the bedroom.

Grimacing, eyes wet, Timothy hunched over, hugging the casted arm to his waist. ''That was dumb. I think I broke the bone again.'' He dropped into the nearest chair, a stray from the kitchen set, which happened to be between Maxey and the front door. ''Everything I've done lately is dumb.''

''You want me to take you to the emergency room and find out? If the bone needs to be reset, I mean.''

He shook his bowed head.

Maxey chewed at her bottom lip. If Sam was at headquarters, it would take about five minutes, even with the siren, to get to this end of Spruce Street. Five minutes didn't seem like an insurmountable time for her to have to hold on to life for dear life.

''So, Timothy, did you ever decide what kind of car to buy?''

He sat up a little straighter and cautiously shook his arm, still not looking at Maxey. ''I knew the forensic wizards would sniff out traces of fiberglass. That's why I set Celia on fire.''

His flat, matter-of-fact tone made the words especially horrible. The truth lay out in the open between them, a malevolent genie that could never be forced back into its bottle.

Maxey quietly rearranged her legs, setting one foot on the floor in order to give herself a push-off start if necessary. ''Why? Why did you hit me?'' She gingerly touched the side of her head, where the scab felt stiff and scaly. ‘‘Because I’m a Komodo dragon?’’

Timothy’s wan smile rechanneled the paths of his tears. He fumbled a wad of handkerchief out of a back pocket of his shorts and scrubbed at his face with it. ‘‘It was so perfect there for a while, Chet taking the rap. I let myself think it was over. Even if Celia wakes up, who’s going to credit what she might say?’’

‘‘Why do you suppose Chet confessed to crimes he didn’t commit?’’

Timothy slumped in the chair, studying the crumpled handkerchief. ‘‘He hated himself. He hated his life. He was mourning his sister and his job. Everything made him crazy. He wanted to kill someone, and someone had been killed; ergo, he was guilty.’’ Timothy glanced up, meeting Maxey’s eyes. ‘‘I got an A in Psychology One-oh-one.’’

‘‘It really *was* you he saw with Celia in the Gunderloy yard the evening she was attacked.’’

‘‘After I’d talked to the funeral director, I drove over there to look at the place. She caught me as I went out the back door. She was taking a shortcut through the yard to go up to Applewood Street with her damn clipboard, looking for signatures to her petition. She thought since I had a key, I must be from Skye and Skye, and she lit into me, calling me all kinds of names and giving me little shoves, like she wanted to push me off the face of the earth.’’

Maxey breathed shallowly, seeing the two of them squared off in the twilight, a foolhardy terrier yapping at a deceptively passive bear.

"So to shut her up, I said, 'I'm not a realtor; I'm the owner.' Big mistake." Timothy snorted. "She just went on and on about what my responsibilties were. Save the house. Blah, blah, blah. Every time I tried to get away, she'd grab my sleeve and talk some more."

"But you didn't have to hit her," Maxey said softly. "You could have just pushed her away."

"I tried. She swung the clipboard at me, and she missed and fell on one knee with her back to me, and I was just so mad, so mad. . . ."

For a moment, silence hung in the room. No sirens keened.

"Damn it, Maxey, I didn't want to preserve a stupid old house. I wanted lots and lots of money."

For a few hopeful seconds, Maxey did hear a siren, but it was only Moe in the next room, voicing unease at the bad vibes his kitty sensors were picking up.

"When I thought she was dead, I panicked. I was afraid the cops could tell she'd been hit by a fiberglass club, and how many of those are there around? So I dragged her up to the deserted property overlooking the Gunderloy, and I burned—" He swiped the handkerchief around his face and neck again.

''Fire kind of scares me. That's why I hired Tilton to do it the next time.''

Maxey shut her eyes briefly, feeling sick. ''You hit me, same as Celia, because you were afraid I'd somehow discover and expose you. And you tied me up and left me to die, expecting the arson would finish off what you'd started.''

''Finish you both off—you and the Gunderloy. Only you've got more lives than a . . . a . . . Komodo dragon.'' Timothy stood up, and Maxey couldn't help flinching. ''Anything else you want to know, Maxey? The murderer always confesses to his prospective victim before he does her in.''

Timothy walked into the kitchen, drew a drink of water from the tap, chugged it down, and returned to the chair. All the while, Maxey's eyes scanned the living room, searching for a defensive weapon.

I don't even have a bra on, she thought. Her throat percolated a small, sobbing laugh.

''You're so bright, Timothy. You should have realized that your hitting Celia wasn't premeditated. A good lawyer could have gotten you off with hardly any prison time.''

''Maxey, Maxey. You know that isn't true. Because it wasn't my first such offense.''

She wanted to cover her ears, hide her eyes, shake her head in vehement denial. Instead, she watched Timothy and waited for the rest of the story to violate her mind.

"Money. It's all about money. I wanted to walk into a store and buy anything without having to give something else up that month. A car, an armload of books—even just a lousy carton of good ice cream, for Christ's sake." Timothy drew a shuddering breath and stared into space past Maxey's shoulder. "She was old, and all her best times were done and gone. What did she have to look forward to except pain and decline?"

Maxey wrapped herself in both arms, trying to keep the horror out of her face.

"You told me how to do it, Maxey. You told me about the rash of runaway vehicles around town. So the day of the concert, I scouted up Baseline till I found a couple of parked cars that were old enough that they didn't have power steering or brakes."

Maxey frowned.

"You can't steer with the motor off if the car's equipped with power steering," Timothy explained. "The VW bus wasn't even locked, so that was my first choice, though I could have used a piece of wire or just busted a window to get in, if I had to." He sat forward, elbows on knees, studying the floor between his tennis shoes. "After the concert, I nipped up the street and steered the VW down to where I'd left her standing. Just before the impact, I rolled out of the front seat." With his thumbnail, he picked at the damaged spot on the cast. "I landed on my arm wrong. Otherwise, I was in good shape. And in the dark and confusion, it was easy to make everyone believe I'd been running toward my grandmother when the bus rolled into her.''

Now Maxey heard the siren, far away, fading in and out on the breeze.

Timothy raised his head. If he heard Maxey's help approaching, he gave no sign. ''I like you, Maxey. I didn't want to kill you. But now it sort of seems like the thing to do. I mean, why should you go on living free and happy when it's your fault I'm in prison and unhappy?'' This time when he stood up, he moved toward the couch.

''No, listen, Timothy. Timothy!'' she shrieked as his left arm drew back and began to swing around at her, the cast a pale, ponderous blur.

Rolling sideways, she felt the blow thump the back of the couch and smelled dust. Her momentum carried her off the edge of the seat to land hard on both knees. Above her, Timothy was doubled over, struggling to lift his weighted arm out of the couch back. Maxey scuttled on hands and knees toward the kitchen, scrambled upright, and lunged to free the butcher knfe from its rack on the wall. Before she could turn around, Timothy's two arms dropped around her shoulders, pinning her arms and the knife to her sides.

''Gotcha!'' he chortled, dragging her toward the front door. ''Drop the knife.''

''Timothy—''

"Drop it! You know you wouldn't use it, anyway." His hug tightened, squeezing the air out of her lungs and leaving no room for the next breath. She dropped the knife.

Timothy's injured arm let go of her, and he fumbled to open the front door. Over the sound of their grunts and shuffling feet, Sam's siren wailed ever closer.

"You're my hostage." Timothy panted in her ear. He yanked the door wide, knocking it against the wall. "Help me get away and I'll turn you loose in Mexico or someplace. Come on, Maxey. Be a sport."

Across the brief landing, the stairs fell away in front of them. Bracing her feet, leaning backward, hard, into Timothy's greater strength, Maxey felt a mixture of terror and rage.

"It's over, Timothy," she shouted at him. "Don't do anything else dumb!"

He paused. The struggle came to a full stop just short of the threshold while both of them listened to Sam's siren fill the stairwell and cut off in midhowl.

Maxey felt Timothy take one deep breath. His grip on her loosened and then he pushed her—not toward the stairs, but sideways, so viciously that she couldn't keep her footing. She sprawled full length along the kitchen floor, bare arms squealing against the linoleum. When she raised up on an elbow and looked back the length of her body, Timothy was retreating from the open door, his face as pale and expressionless as milk.

A car door slammed and running footsteps pounded.

Having backed to the middle of Maxey's living room, Timothy stopped, tilted his head back, and blinked at the ceiling. His eyes stretched open, then squeezed tightly shut. His mouth expelled a wordless, wailing protest. Like a sprinter off the block, arms and legs pumping high, he ran at the open door.

Scrambling up too late to intercept him as he hurtled across the room, Maxey howled in protest, too, as Timothy launched himself through the doorway and, into the maw of the stairwell. Feet still pumping wildly, a broad jumper going for a record, Timothy hung for a moment before gravity hauled him down.

Maxey twisted away before she could see him hit, but she couldn't shut out the sound. It went on and on, a crashing, cracking, splashing avalanche. Finally, the house quieted, and she could hear herself crying and Sam shouting from the bottom of the echoing oak-walled chasm.

Epilogue

■ ■ ■

At five till six on a crisp Tuesday evening in early September, Maxey walked into the marble and granite municipal building at Broadway and Canyon, notebook in hand, to cover the city council meeting for the *Regard.*

Several loose knots of civic-minded citizens murmured in the hall outside the chamber. As Maxey passed one of these little groups, a hand snaked out and attached itself lightly to her forearm.

''Hey. When are we going to have our dinner celebration?'' Calen Taylor stepped away from four other men, and they went on talking without him. He wore a blue-gray suit, a white shirt, a red tie, and a new beard as neat as a closely cropped lawn.

Maxey returned his smile. ''You really want to do it? Call me at the office tomorrow and we'll compare calendars.''

''Deal.''

She glanced around the barren, colorless hall. "You come here often?"

"I'm speaking to the council tonight about the fire department budget."

"I'll clap and whistle whenever you pause for a breath." Through the open double doors, Maxey could see the council members taking their seats behind the massive walnut desk. "Where did you get your agenda?" she asked, nodding at the stapled sheaf of white papers in his hand.

"Over by the—whoops, looks like they're all gone. Sit by me and we'll share." He touched her elbow in a gesture of old-fashioned chivalry, as if she needed help negotiating the double doors.

The padded auditorium seat sighed as Maxey sat down. Calen handed her the agenda, which he'd rolled like a diploma for easy holding. She flattened it on her knees as the mayor called the meeting to order. There it was—item one on the top page: "Public Hearing and Final Reading on the Ordinance to Rezone Applewood Street and Nebraska Street from Broadway West to Single-Family Residential. . . ."

Maxey nudged Calen. "Did you know about this?"

He squinted at where she pointed on the agenda, shrugged, and shook his head, obviously not that interested.

Maxey half-rose from her seat and craned to look

around at the audience. She spotted Bailey Marker near the back, and Charles Skye, Jr., front row, center.

The mayor was already calling for the public to speak on this ordinance, and a tall, thin woman with a short hairdo like gray cotton candy stepped to the lectern and cleared her throat.

"My name is Arlene McChristian, and I live at Two-oh-eight Nebraska Street. I represent the neighborhood group, all the homeowners on Nebraska and Applewood streets. They picked me to talk to you, because"—here, Mrs. McChristian, who'd been reading from an index card, shuffled it to the bottom of a little stack and consulted the next three-by-five card—"right now, my house is the only one on either of the two streets that is not a single-family dwelling. Everyone thought that if you saw I'm in favor of rezoning, you'd pass the ordinance."

Belatedly, Maxey opened her notebook and began to scribble notes at high speed. Calen opened a notebook of his own and stared down at it, apparently studying his upcoming speech.

"I don't happen to have any renters in my upstairs apartment right now, so this is a good time to stop being a landlady. That's always been more trouble than what it's worth. My renters are usually college students who don't have any money, and I get so tired of asking for the rent every—"

Mrs. McChristian had apparently slipped off into

an adlib mode. Recollecting herself, she continued. "We want our quiet little part of town to stay that way. A condominium at the end of the two streets would bring in more than twice the traffic, along with its concomitant noise pollution and noxious fumes. The unfortunate fire that destroyed the Gunderloy house—"

Maxey looked up from her writing, flexing her fingers. Charles Skye sat sideways, arm draped over the back of his chair, intently listening. His brown hair gleamed; his tan glowed; his pinkie ring sparkled.

"—all the more aware of our wonderful architectural heritage. And so we ask that the council help us to preserve the historic character of our neighborhood by rezoning it to single-family residential. Thank you."

"Thank you, Mrs. McChristian. The next person signed up to speak is Mr. Charles Skye."

While he strode to the lectern, Maxey turned to scan the audience again, and when he began his statement, she settled back, disappointed.

His hands in his pockets, Skye spoke to the council earnestly, man to man, incorporating lots of eye contact. "You have a seven-page proposal in your packets, gentlemen, that reiterates what I said at the first reading of this proposed ordinance. You'll find there the tax-revenue figures that our forty-unit condominium would generate for the city. I won't insult you by reading them over to you now—you know how to read, and you know what those dollar amounts could do for Boulder's long-term economy.''

Skye and Skye had run a full-page ad in the *Regard* every week since the first one in June. The dollar amounts had done a lot for the newspaper's long-term economy. At this moment, Maxey felt corrupted, unclean. No matter how Reece balked and pleaded, she would wash their hands of Skye Development tomorrow.

''Not only do I represent the interests of the city of Boulder; I represent, tonight, the interests of Mrs. Mary Ann Jessup, who may be many miles distant in Florida but who wants to do what's right for this community, wants to see it grow and prosper.''

Maxey had been writing rent checks to Mary Ann, a cousin of a cousin of Timothy's mother. Just what Boulder needed—another absentee landlord.

Charles Skye pleaded eloquently half a minute past his allotted time, and then Bailey Marker gave a gruff, brief rebuttal. No one else wanted to speak, but the council spent several minutes ramifying, factoring, interpellating, caviling, and opining.

Then they voted to rezone Skye and Skye out of the equation.

Maxey couldn't sit still. Handing back Calen's agenda and mouthing, See you, she threaded her way between seats to escape into the cooler hall. Most of the neighborhood group had exited ahead of her.

They milled together, whispering and quietly laughing.

"Excuse me please," Maxey said, squeezing between two tall, corpulent gentlemen as she tried to reach Bailey.

The men stepped aside, letting her through, and she saw the face she'd been watching for all evening. A raw-pink forehead, tea-colored eyes without eyebrows, and a set smile that listed a little to the left. A multicolored gypsy scarf was artfully braided and tied to cover her head.

Maxey hugged her with care, not sure what parts of her still hurt. "I'm so glad you're here to see this victory, Celia."

"How does that old joke go? I'm glad to be anywhere."

Bailey patted Maxey's shoulder. "We're going to try to buy the Gunderloy property from the Florida woman and make it into a pocket park."

Maxey touched the slight indentation above her right ear. "Put me down for fifty bucks."